Harold The Imp

JOSEPH BARONE

All Small Tales
© 2014 Joseph Barone

Cover Art by Jessica Peak

Layout by Ryan Leyba

Dedicated to my mother Claire Barone,
who taught me how to be human.

A Special Thank You to my wife Sabrina Barone,
sister Alessandra and father Peter for their constant support
and understanding, and for the dream-makers listed below,
without whom this endeavor could not have been realized:

Nancy D'Aietti Romano
Bryan Abdelnoor
Joe Pellicone
Kathryn Dworak
Bertha Penenori

CONTENTS

PROLOGUE

Bruella was gathering a cauldron of snow to boil. It would take several hours to heat up and once it did she would throw in some frozen potatoes for dinner. The potatoes were stored in bulk near the firewood behind the tiny cottage. Dried herbs were kept in linen bags for just a dash of flavor- the winters are long and no one knows how infrequently good meals might come. One must ration their sense of taste. Salt was out of the question as it fetched a full copper penny at the market.

This is an unfortunate bane of humans, I thought as I observed them from afar- the necessity to rely on powers greater than themselves. Often, those powers conspire against them. The cold and the ice provide a little bit, and take away a lot. Bruella's husband Hansel returned from his daily forage, leaving the relative comfort of his frozen cottage for only a half hour at a time.

As usual in the winter months, he'd brought back very little of value: some kindling bark, twigs, and rare grimmle-berries that grow in winter. The berries were for him and not Bruella, nor for their hungry children, Hans and Adelaide. Watching him these past few days, I saw that he was no monster. He'd share food with them once he was sated, but as things go, merriment and foodstuffs were scarce, and a not-so-good man appears even worse in the face of that.

He looked at his crippled father, who lived with them. Another mouth to feed. Another mouth, connected to a body, withered and unable to assist in any way. "Feeling well, old man?" he asked as a courtesy, and an accusation.

"Indeed I am in excellent health, my son. Albeit I cannot walk, you know. I never thought I would live to such an extreme age. Forty-five years old. It must be those modern potions concocted by those newfangled alchemists. I drank an elixir once which had...fallen off the wagon of a traveling merchant, and I have now outlived all of my friends."

"And all of your welcome," Hansel muttered under breath. Bruella gave her husband a stern look as she was churning the snow by hand with a wooden broom.

"Now Hansel, it's not Poppa's fault he's lived so long and seen so much. We should all be this lucky. Why, in our day and age it is a miracle to have two surviving children past the age of ten." She turned to them, just barely 10 and 11, respectively. "When will you two find someone to marry and give me grandchildren?"

Poppa scratched his head, making a bristly sound against the coarse grain of his hair. "What year is it again?"

Bruella stopped churning for a moment. "Fourteen hundred something? Maybe fifteen hundred something...it's an age in which practically no one knows what year it is. We're just lucky to have teeth."

Hansel sighed and sat down on his favorite chair, which was his only chair. It was termite-eaten, but it served its function. He looked over at his children and his father. Were that they were all termite-eaten and yet serve a function. Hansel's despair showed in deep grooves of his face. He looked at his plump wife, who remained plump throughout the year no matter how much or how little food there was in the harvest.

PROLOGUE

She had dark, long black hair and wore a yellow frock, which started out as a white frock, many years ago on their wedding day. Adelaide and Hans played together in the middle of the cottage in front of the fireplace. They played a children's game with stems of hay, making believe they were field workers who spent countless hours turning soil and planting their crops.

The wine had turned to vinegar this year but Hansel still drank it. The bitter acrid flavor of it served to make his life appear slightly less bitter by comparison. The only thing of value in his life, he thought, was in his pocket. I'd followed him long enough to know the man. He wore his thoughts not just in his facial expressions or words but in the very air surrounding him, which often smelled of pride. And body odor.

He reached into the right flap on his pant leg and pulled out an iron ring. It looked like iron, but may have been tarnished silver. The ring had a gemstone that looked unimpressive perhaps to a prince, but to a commoner and a pauper, it held a particular thrall. The gem appeared to be glass, very scuffed up and weathered by time.

Earlier in the year a merchant in the town square offered half a king's ransom for the ring. Hansel had shown it to him to boast about his greatest sole possession, and declined the man's offer. "But it will make you financially secure, you and your family would never need to go hungry again. And the winters are long, you know."

Laughter preceded a sneer. "I never go hungry, no matter how long the winters are. The ring is not for sale."

Hansel's thoughts were interrupted by his children's bickering over their game.

"If you till the soil too much, the ground won't be able to grow carrots!"

"If you don't till the soil enough, the ground won't grow anything!"

Something shattered inside of Hansel. "Enough, all of you!

You play games about work, but you never work. You all want, want, want, but none of you gives! Except you, Bruella, bless your heart. But we are dying, we are all dying! Do you not see how you slay me with your idleness? I shall not go to ground and allow you to be the death of me. You are imps, all of you. Imps, I say!"

Imps. Such an accusation could not be a coincidence. It was my cue to enter, perhaps. Hansel put on a scarf and hat. Bruella asked, "Where are you going? There is a storm coming- look at the gray sky and the snow now falling!"

Hansel snickered at her as well. "There is an ale house two kilometers away. I mean to go there or have my death of the cold. Either one would suit me fine." She stared at him frumpishly. He looked back at her sheepishly. "We haven't any wine. I am in need of drink. Should the storm make my return impassable, I shall return a bit later than I expect."

He slammed the door but didn't need to; there were no hinges after all and it never fully closed anyway. I let him walk a while, observing him from a safe distance. The poor eyesight of man and in fact all the paltry human senses astound me. It is beautiful how they make due with so few faculties. With eyesight worse than a predatory bird, an archer can hit a far-off target without needing to see it as well. It is beautiful to do so much with so little. And yet, those possessed of magical or political power tend to do so little with so much.

The snow began to fall slowly and lightly on the ground. It was nice. Fresh. The air was crisp and promising. I considered putting out my pipe before approaching him, but decided I would allow him to see it. None but wealthy merchants or aristocracy could afford to smoke anything but burnt leaves.

"Ho there, good sir. How goes it?"

"It goes." Hansel sped up his gait.

"It looks like a blizzard is coming. Do you not fear being caught in these woods when the worst of it comes?"

Without missing a beat, "You seem not to have a care in the world, smoking your pipe in the storm. I know these woods like I know my wife's face. I need not fear." He did not slow down.

"Perhaps you do need fear. There are things in the woods that are frightening. Wild animals. Hunters. Uncanny spirits, disturbed by the dark magic of winter, frothing about in the air like agitated water. Perhaps you need fear them."

He slowed down but only slightly. He looked into the sky, as if to mete out the clouds from the spirits which float on the air. Seeing none, his attention turned back to the darkening road ahead.

I appeared in front of him quicker than a gust of wind. He stopped walking. "You have something of mine, Hansel." I put a strong hand on his shoulder and squeezed it gently, like a friend would do. I did not want to frighten him. "You don't know that it belongs to me. You believe it belongs to you. But I would like to pay you handsomely for the chance to have it back." I was usually not so direct. Deception is my nature and well, honesty is a greater policy, I am told.

"I have nothing. I come from nothing. Go along on your way, whomever or whatever you are."

Smiling, I told him, "You don't come from nothing and you don't have nothing. You have a ring in your pocket. It may be in your possession but it is not yours. I'm sure we can work something out which is beneficial to the both of us. I could not help note the poor quality of your clothing or the shabby nature of your cottage. I can change this for you- I am very old, and very wealthy."

He sneered audibly. "No." He was not afraid of me. I never relied on fear, anyway. Honesty might be a good policy, but it is not my policy. My nature is different. At times dishonest means make honest ends, and so there is comfort in the gray of life if you are a moral person. Few are.

The snow began to fall a bit heavier as the temperature

dropped. It did not bother me too much, and in any case I was well clothed. I could see my new friend trembling a bit but his pride held him steady.

I extended a gloved hand to him. "My name is Harold."

He shook it with a bare hand. "Hansel. But maybe you knew that."

"Yes I did. I also know you're headed to Loggerheads Ale House, two kilometers that way." I pointed to an unmade road under a sad sky. "You seek to imbibe until you forget what you consider to be a miserable and pathetic life. Which is why I understand how closely you cling to my ring."

"My ring."

"I see. Well, we both disagree on this one little point, but it doesn't mean that we can't be civil." I pulled out a full leather flask of wine. "I am chilled to the bone myself. Will you let me into your cottage and share this wine with me? My kind looks favorably upon those who show us friendship. A friend of mine is a friend for life."

He looked slightly uneasy- not frightened, but not sure where I was going with this. He was unsure of my intentions but I was quite sure of his.

"Relax. If I wanted to rob you, I'd have robbed you by now. If I wanted to do worse- well, I'd have done it. You needn't worry. Please, share a drink and some hospitality. I swear my friendship on my honor. My kind, as subversive as we might be, sticks to their word."

I should have bribed him with the wine to begin with, rather than money. Money would have been useless until the weather changed and he was able to spend it. But wine, that is a readily useable thing. As old as I am and as close as I feel to humans, I will never learn or remember everything there is to know about them. That would take several of my lifetimes.

His pride gave way to desire. It was not my intention to tempt him, only to befriend him and get the chance to finally meet his family after watching from afar. I should say that it was indeed cold and getting colder. I was not made of fire; some shelter would truly be welcome.

He raised his hand palm up, towards the shabby home. It was his version of a kind gesture. "What is your kind, anyway? Must be a kind that can wield magic- you don't look so old to me."

Indeed I don't. "I can appear as I wish, more or less. I have noticed my true form is a bit more frightening to people. So I mask it with a handsome young face. Call it vanity."

We walked in further silence. I was amused since I could almost feel his curiosity weighing on him.

My boots scrunched the tight snow below my feet. My companion's feet were practically bare. It is a shame. Hansel had a better ancestry than this.

We arrived back in five minutes. Hansel opened the door. Bruella was still stirring the snow, which had mostly turned to slurry water. The potatoes were near her feet close to the crude fireplace, around which the entire cottage was built. The sturdiest object in the home was the fireplace and chimney. All else was flimsy. The roof was made of straw and the walls were cracked wood.

The home was humble and meek, and others from low status tend to be the same way. And yet Hansel was not that way; it was not his policy. Boastful, prideful, angry- this was the serum in his blood. It is truly a shame that few means do not always breed gracious people. I believe it is a gift to have less. And on the other side, it is a blessing for a rich person to grow a love of others, which that person then has the means to act upon.

"I'm back. I've missed you all. Bruella, this is my friend Harold. Add in an extra potato for him. You like boiled potato, don't you Harold? We have no salt."

She regarded me with a smile and a curtsy. "I wasn't expecting company. How delightful."

7

I kissed her hand. "Hansel and I bumped into each other in the forest. He saw how bad the weather was getting and graciously offered me some shelter until the storm passes."

She giggled, apparently proudly surprised about her husband's goodness, and grabbed another potato to put in front of the fireplace.

I shook my head. "No, thank you, I've already eaten and am full. But please, go on and eat."

Bruella was not beautiful, but there was something beautiful about her. "This pot is so big that it will take three hours to boil, and thank goodness, it does that all by itself." She motioned for me to sit on the only seat in the cottage but I declined. I looked down. The ground was made of frozen dirt.

"I'll stand, thank you."

She looked around, trying to find something to put away or clean, unused as she probably was to hosting a guest. She stopped abruptly. "So, you're my husband's...friend? I didn't know my husband had any. You'll have to excuse the mess."

"Nonsense, these are lovely quarters. Yes, I'm Hansel's friend. He has spoken to me about you all. You must be Bruella." I kissed her greasy black hand. "And you two beautiful children must be Hans and Adelaide," I waved. Hansel looked confused. He hadn't told me their names.

"And that must be Poppa. Don't get up," I joked. Poppa was on the large communal bed whose mattress was- just like the roof- straw.

I turned back to Hansel. He was nibbling on grimmle-berries.

"I will tell you a secret about grimmle-berries later, before I go. They are far more special than just delicious snacks." He kept chewing. "Can I see my ring? I should love to gaze upon it once more. Even though I can't possess it any longer, it gives me comfort to know it is in good hands."

Hansel reached into his pocket and then tossed it to me. "It is my ring. Not yours. You can hold it for a minute."

I held it. It was lighter than it looked. Dirty. Hansel hadn't cleaned it since he inherited it from his mother. I turned it over and over, marveling at it, fingering the glass stone gem. I tossed it back to Hansel, who plucked it deftly from the air.

Bruella finally decided what she'd offer me as host. "Can I get you some...snow...to drink? It'll only take a few minutes to melt." I produced the wine flask from my jacket and patted it to show it was full. I handed it to Hansel who was more than willing to take it from me.

Looking over at the children and observing their constant state of insatiation, I took out a few cinnamon sticks for them. Their faces alighted with an appreciative glow- the virtue of the meek. They politely lined up and waited their turn to be handed the candy. Hansel by comparison was already taking long gulps straight from the flask.

"This wine is of great vintage," he said, almost to himself. He certainly was not complimenting me.

For Bruella I had brought a new white apron. "I apologize for the sexism, but we are still in the dark ages."

She shook her head with a tear in her eye. "Not at all. It is beautiful. Thank you. How is it that you are friends--" she looked at a rapidly inebriating Hansel-- "with him?"

I laughed. Hansel closed the top of the flask, apparently sated. Or embarrassed. "Well, it is a long answer to a short question. It all has to do with that little ring. Would you like to hear my story while the water for your dinner boils?"

The children, Bruella and even Poppa inclined towards me, arranging themselves around me in a circle. Hansel continued sitting in his chair, but his quiet attention was on me.

"It happened almost a century ago..."

CHAPTER 1

I am an Imp. That is, I'm a mischievous creature known to play pranks and tricks, who wields quite a bit of magic, but only deceptive magic. I cannot cast a hex or make a potion or anything like that, but I can do other things. My form, and that of all imps can change at will, although this ability and all of our other ones require tedious learning. Any skill we possess can take decades to perfect.

Our physicality is much like that of humans humans except for two obvious differences: some imps are red-colored with gray eyes, and some imps are gray-colored with red eyes. I am the kind that is red with gray eyes. All imps are male, just like all witches are female. When we fall in love (which is rare), it is with other creature types. How do we have children, you ask? They are born from our unions with women of other realms; we are all halflings of a single heart.

An important and hurtful myth that I must address is this: We do not have horns or hooves; we are not demons, though sometimes the difference between mischief and malice can be a very thin filament.

Mischief is in my nature, it is in my blood. But one's blood can change. It can boil, it can become thin; it can also thicken and flow backward sometimes. Blood is not stone, and yet even stone can be transformed.

I've heard it philosophized that my kind is mischievous because we are powerful, and we grow bored with the world. We must therefore add flavor to our lives since a bland palate is a fate worse than death. Trickery is our favorite sport and is in fact all that we know.

Perhaps we do what we do out of boredom, but not through consideration of our power. As I said, we are not physically strong. Our success relies on our ability to influence outcomes by influencing people, and our magic helps us elicit the right response from them. In that sense we are very powerful.

My skin is flesh- it would tear and rip from stabbing, would singe and burn with fire. We are mortal, so far as I know. This does not hinder us in any way, however. A swordsman will have a difficult time slaying me if I project the illusion of hundreds of myself around him. I can make myself appear to be an army and though he'd best me in a one-on-one swordfight, he'd think he was surrounded, thereby stifling his attack in the first place.

A lion would think twice about ripping my throat out if I looked like a much bigger lion to him. It is a deception but not a reality. But the reality does not matter, if the illusion is powerful enough. Should that lion disregard his fear and attack me in that situation, I'd be dead. But we imps know how others are most likely to react. We observe people keenly, especially in the first century of our lives. In that time, we have toyed and played and tested the waters, and so learned how best to fool. We know the outcomes our actions are likeliest to elicit- what works and what doesn't.

A young imp, less than a couple of centuries old, usually appears as a child looking for a friend in strangers. He will use deception as a means to gain camaraderie, which is usually a friendship doomed to fail. Not understanding that others are less tricksy, the imp will inevitably do something wrong, play a game which their new friends don't like, and it will cause them to part ways in a most upsetting fashion. Rejection is well known and well feared among us.

Older imps may sometimes interact more deeply in human affairs. They are better adapted to people and can manipulate them far better. This can lead to ever greater, more complex games. Typically they will join humans in their affairs and elevate themselves to high standing. They may become court jesters, palace astrologers or royal advisors. Their proximity to power without actually having it, feels like catnip does to felines. Impnip perhaps. It's intoxicating to control the horses without holding the reins. When the carriage falls off a cliff, it is the driver's fault, not the one who whispers in the driver's ear.

And I am a very old imp, the oldest one I know. Long life does something to you, makes you see things differently, no matter what kind of creature you are. At some point you have tasted every flavor, seen every kind of sunset and sunrise, every snowfall, sunshower, storm, earthquake, every phase of the moon. There is always something more to see and learn, but the mystery cannot help but pale and fade. Humans do not understand and hopefully will never understand, the sorrow that comes with singular power and longevity.

In love, they pledge themselves to one another "forever." If only they could taste the smallest morsel of forever, they'd measure their words. I've walked among you all, and for many, forever ends so quickly. It is easy to pledge forever when life is snuffed out so fast. And yet, for some, love truly can last. For some, forever is not a lie. Some spirits hold hands while watching the mountains rise and fall, and that is only a single day for them.

For myself, the idea of forever made me cold. I became angry that I could not connect to anyone without deceiving them. I did not mean harm or ill to anyone, but my ways inevitably bring darkness and vexation. I yearned to transform myself and my ways into something better. To explain, I will quickly recount the tale of The Horsefly.

There was a horsefly on a farm, who spent every day in and day out buzzing in the ears of the horses in the stable. Though it was the horsefly's nature to bug the horses, he did not like being vexing to them. He'd rather be friends with them than annoy them. However, buzzing in ears was his nature and alas he was a slave to his ways. He could do nothing else than vex.

One day a very patient horse told the horsefly about some trouble the farmer was having with the bears. The bears were stealing all the honey from the bees and there was none left for the farmer to sell at the market. Winter was still months away but at this rate there would be no honey in anyone's larders in the entire town that season.

The horsefly thought it over and devised a clever solution. Instead of using his gifts for ill- that is, the vexation of the horses, he would get all his annoying friends together and use their combined bugging ability to shoo away the bears.

The next day when the bears went to dip into the honey pot, they were attacked by thousands of small horseflies, who nipped and buzzed at them in a furious fervor. The bears didn't like that. They roared and growled but the flies did not relent. They simply buzzed even harder. The bears couldn't take it any more, so they fled, never to return to such an annoying place again.

The honey pot was forever safe, and therefore the farmer and townspeople were happy. The horseflies decided to go deep into the forest to bug the bears rather than stay at the farm and bug the horses and so the horses were happy to no longer be vexed.

I am like that horsefly. Irritating, subversive. Clever. And desiring to be different than what I am. At least the horsefly was able to translate his natural impulses into something good.

About a century ago, I began to brood in silence. No longer taken to pranks or Impnip, I withdrew into the realm of the

Imps, which is called Monello. It takes ages and lengths of human lifetimes for magical creatures to change, if they do at all. We don't get bored as quickly as people because we live longer than they do. And our nature is our nature. We don't typically seek to counter it like the people do.

Like the rivers that flow downstream without questioning their direction, magical creatures live their lives adhering to their ways. For me to withdraw from prank-pulling was not ordinary, of course. My brother Erumite came to my side. He sought to recruit me on a scam. Sometimes scams are big and sometimes they are small. They're fun either way.

Erumite is among the most spritely and effervescent imps in all of imp-dom. He is always excited to pull a scheme. When he is not pulling one, he is planning one. He lives for the excitement, the thrill, the unmitigated pleasure of the hunt.

Now, before I go into detail about the conversation with my brother, let me explain about Monello and also about the kinds of scams we pull.

Monello is our realm, a hidden kingdom which sits just outside of the forest. Imps walk through the door between realms as we please. We are not very communal and prefer the company of humans over each other. We find each other annoying, to be quite honest, but that works well when we act together to pull something off.

There are not very many imps in the world and although our natures are the same, our personalities are different. The schemes we plan therefore reflect those different personalities. We may pull tricks alone or together, but never with more than four imps. That's simply too many.

I'd had a great time in my day, especially as a royal advisor and court astrologer. I showed King Leonard of a nearby kingdom that I was capable of magic, so he trusted me to advise him about everything. Troop positions, kingdom policy, matters of justice, personal things- anything you can imagine.

Therefore you can also imagine all the wonderful, terrible things that were possible. I told him he must cluck like a chicken every hour on the hour, even at night, in order to protect his kingdom from raiders for 75 years. He awoke every hour on the hour, for I awoke him and at my urging, he clucked like the biggest and loudest chicken ever farmed in history. I don't normally sleep, but I do laugh.

The whole king's court, therefore went without sleep for the month that I played that trick. Next I told him his clothes were invisible, for the finest tailor in the land had made them. But they were not- he was simply naked. Again, he and the entire king's court walked around naked for a month. As an aside, I'm shopping for an author to write that story for me.

The queen of this kingdom was very rude, very superior. She'd thought herself divine and looked down upon any who were not royal themselves. Therefore in the dead of night, I switched her newborn child with the newborn child of one of her lowliest subjects. I laughed to myself each time she suckled the child, and when he became king of that land, I decided to retire as advisor. It was the perfect culmination of my time there.

I gave the lowly subject whose child I switched five pieces of the finest king's gold, and her "son" became a learned healer and philosopher through the education that it bought.

As I was saying earlier, Erumite, my brother, called on me to assist in a common scam. Scams are somewhat different than pranks, and pranks are different than tricks. You can refer to them all interchangeably, but in truth there are subtle delineations.

"Come on, brother. You have been cooped up in Monello for too long. There is nothing to do here, no fun to be had. You cannot spend the rest of your long life away from your nature. The nature that we both share. Ours is destiny. Frivolous, fickle, random, nonsensical destiny. A destiny which does not know from whence it comes."

CHAPTER 1

In truth he was right, at least as far as Monello is concerned. It is a bleak, dreary place. There is nothing to do but dream up better, greater schemes. It is a place to retire after pulling off big schemes. We do sleep, but only once we've reached apex. The culmination of long cons, scams, tricks, pranks, can bring us into a kind of hibernation. It is a satisfied sleep.

The scheme Erumite planned was to scam a man from his late brother's inheritance by claiming that the brother owed a large debt to us. Two of us would be creditors and two of us would be magistrates. We have no need of money, but we do enjoy when we trick humans out of theirs. This ensures we have large stores of mostly useless gold and jewels. It comes in handy at times. Bribery of public officials can be fun.

I agreed and we transported ourselves to the mourning man. I was a magistrate. Erumite was a creditor. The other two imps were also old, seasoned veterans- brothers Chigga and Chiggu.

The man who lost his brother- Jack, was driving a carriage. Jack wore a black tunic and tousled hair. He looked sad, down-trodden. This was going to be hilarious, my nature said, excitedly. Another part of me hated what we were about to do.

We were in our own carriage, driven by a horse that we stole from Jack's brother's estate. We rode alongside him, me at the helm and Erumite by my side. I called out, "Excuse me, young sir, yes you there. Would you perchance know where I can find Jack Gutten, brother of Gus?"

His carriage came to a halt as he pulled on the reins, to which I responded in kind. "I am Jack- what business do you have with me?"

Erumite jumped in as he is wont to do. "I am here to denounce you to the local magistrate. You see, Gus owed me and several others a considerable fortune, which I am collecting on their behalf."

Jack swallowed hard. "Gus was a mill worker his entire life. He had a pittance for himself and his family- how can he possibly be so indebted that you call what he owes a 'fortune'?"

Erumite was a fine actor. "Gus was friends with his banker, who gave him loans he had no business giving. That banker was my employee and he was hung last Tuesday once I discovered he'd been stealing from me. I am the bank owner and lost a considerable sum thanks to your brother and his friend."

To my eyes Jack appeared devastated from his loss to begin with. This was just sugar on the cake. "How much did he owe you?"

"Fifty pieces."

"FIFTY silver pieces? What did he possibly spend that on?"

"Fifty gold pieces, I'm afraid. I do not know what he spent it on but I imagine it was unwholesome."

Jack's expression hardened. "I knew my brother to be a man of honor. And I try to be the same way. If there was some possible method by which I could repay you for his actions, I would. But I could not muster fifty gold pieces in my lifetime."

I stayed quiet and let Erumite continue. The rest of us apparently were not needed on this scheme. "We are reasonable men. We know that you cannot be fully held responsible for another man's crimes and he himself is now dead." Jack cringed at that. "But you can give me whatever your brother left behind."

"All he left in this world is for his wife and young son. Fifteen pieces of silver. That is his entire legacy."

"I'll take it," Erumite said. Perhaps there was no need of a magistrate to intervene in the negotiation. "Fifteen pieces and his debt is forgiven." Not one to let a deal linger, he reached out his hand. Jack shook it weakly. Then he got slowly up and walked into the carriage.

He returned after a long wait with tears in his eyes and handed Erumite a glass jar. "This is everything. Consider the blight on our family name removed."

Erumite took it and pretended to scrutinize each coin. "Yes, this is acceptable. Thank you, Jack, and may you put this terrible truth behind you."

Jack looked back to the carriage. "It soon will be buried in the ground. Thank you, sirs."

I looked back that way. "Do you mean you carry your brother's body with you?"

"Yes. He and I worked together at the mill. When he died of high fever, our employer gave me all my brother's past wages. I bring him back to be buried near his family and to give his widow and son their due. But now unfortunately, I cannot."

"What will become of them?" I asked him. His earnest fear turned something in my stomach sour.

"I shall take them into my own home and care for them myself. We mill workers are of modest means but I will do my best for my family, sir. I am only happy that the bank will look favorably upon us after all this wretchedness."

I turned to Erumite. "Give him back the jar. Now."

He was stupefied. "W-What?"

"I am the magistrate, am I not, young bank owner? My decision has been made. Do it."

Erumite tried to argue with me. I did not appreciate that. "Give Jack his fifteen silver pieces NOW!" I transformed to my usual red color and standard appearance, which bewildered Jack. I grew to enormous proportions to show my brother my rage. "Do not defy me, brother. I command you to give him his rightful due plus ten gold pieces."

Erumite did as he was told, and the other two imps trembled. They'd never seen me that way. I went back to Monello, disdainful of my horrid nature, the one I share with all my kind.

For days I was left alone to sulk and think. I thought about Jack Gutten- the love he had for his family and the nobility of spirit he carried within him. This is possible with humans. It is not possible with us, and I hated myself for being what I was.

My brother came to me to console me. He knew I was troubled with something. And though we tend to be frivolous about everything, we still know fraternal love, albeit frivolously.

Before he could speak to me, I informed him with palm raised, "I intend to leave Monello."

"Shall we go speak in the forest then?"

"I intend to leave it forever."

Erumite blinked in surprise.

"And go where? There are few places in the world as safe as Monello for imps. Do you remember when you went to Arabia five hundred years ago? They imprisoned you in an oil lamp and made you serve its possessor."

"Yes, thank goodness for that Aladdin fellow, who rescued me."

Erumite was smaller than me, and more wiry. He was gray with red eyes. I'd never understood why some of us were a certain color and some of us were a different color. I thought it might have something to do with age- I've noticed the older we get, the redder. But I was born red and never went through a "gray" phase. Most imps preferred to don an outwardly human appearance. Even so, their true form was usually gray. We red imps have become more rare since I was young.

"Where will you go?" he asked me again.

I looked at him with weary gray eyes. "I am tired of being as I am, brother. I wish to be human."

"HUMAN?"

"Yes. There is something beautiful and redeeming about the humans. Although we, and indeed all magical creatures, always follow our nature, humans can choose to overcome it. In that sense they are in greater control of their futures than any of us."

"Then why are they so easy to fool, if they are so great? They haven't the strength of ogres, the wit of imps or the high nobility of Elves. They are fractious, fragmented, and above all, flawed. You are already greater than the greatest of them."

"I am not great. Because I cannot choose to be great. What I am is from birth, not from self-determination or will. In part, I am sorry, brother. Sorry for leaving you all. And yet what I seek is a better, if smaller and shorter, life. I seek to appreciate it. To have flaws to overcome, to find futility, to know love, to know loss, to drink from the flood of human experiences. As I am, I know one thing only- to fool. As a human, both a lesser and a greater world are open to me."

"You cannot change who you are, brother. Only what you are." And with those ominous tidings he left my side in a puff of smoke. Another trick. I didn't prefer to travel that way but I did on occasion.

To be fair, I was considering leaving my post and my people for a long time. But I did not make a firm decision until I spoke to my brother. The loss he felt was more from missing our prankish fun together, than missing me. It is a distinction that a human could certainly comprehend but my people do not. Even I did not understand it at the time.

When he left I gathered my few possessions. I took a jacket, pants, and a satchel. In the satchel I put roughly 100 gold coins. If I was never to return to Monello, then money would help when going out into the world, where gold is worth more than a hundred lives.

I looked down at my ring, which I always wore on my right index finger. The gem was cloudy, a reflection of my turbulent soul. That is, if I had a soul. I didn't know for sure and still don't. I hadn't ever stopped to ponder it, but I knew that humans thought of such things regularly. When mortality is not theoretical, its constant presence is difficult to ignore, I suppose. So there is no end to its rumination.

I changed my appearance to that of a tall, dark man. Harold.

I began my journey by exiting one of Monello's many doors. There was a single guard at each of the doors, in case wanderers strayed into the realm. They were to be escorted out the same way they entered. The guardsmen were more serious imps, except when on holiday.

I decided that for my last exit, I would walk out a door I seldom opened. I knew where I was headed and the door lead me to as direct a path as any. This door was wooden and scratched, unlike most of the other ones which were bronze and ornate. It lead to a clearing in the forest. From there, I had tricks to tell me where to go and how to keep my bearing.

Although my mastery of magic is in the deceptive arts, that does not mean I haven't learned a thing or a thousand along the way. One thing I learned is: bring a jacket and pants. And always appear human to those with whom you wish to speak.

Once I turned the rusty handle and pushed the stubborn hinge I was in the clearing. At the clearing I spotted a pond which collected due to a recent rainfall. This was perfect luck since I could use it as a compass.

The pond was knee-deep, so I waded about a third of the way in. I arranged fallen tree leaves in a circle on the calm surface of the water. Then I plucked out some hairs off of my head and put them in the center of the circle. Finally, I pulled off my ring and rested it on top of my hair.

I whispered, "Find me Vanna and Warlocke." The gem lit up and spun twice, finally pointing in a particular direction. That way. I put the ring back on and kept moving. I could have transported myself far into that direction, but I didn't know exactly where they were.

If I traveled too fast, I could overshoot and the journey could wind up taking more time in the end. So I decided to stroll. I'd have to get used to walking everywhere if I was to be human. No more instant transportation.

It was late summer. But very late summer. The air was brisk with the coming autumn. Grass was part green, part brown, and flowers were approaching their last bloom.

I looked around at some of the flora of the forest. Some of the things I saw grew all year round like moonlock, grimmleberries, pine trees, and trundle herbs. Other things were more seasonal such as hyacinths, daisies, basil, and parsley.

The seasonal plants were waning and the yearlong plants were surviving strong. Soon I'd be picking them from the ground and the trees in order to survive. I'd be hunting and foraging, praying to get through the long winter when it comes. A tear came to my eyes. It sounded so beautiful.

Maybe someday I would find comfort in the love of another. Settle down, have a child, live for him or her. Work hard, grow old, and mete out the end of my days reflecting on my blistered hands and tired back. There could be nothing better.

As I walked through the forest in sublime thoughtfulness, I encountered a fellow imp. I'm unsure if he knew who I was. He was a child, no older than 150 years. As is the wont of young imps, he sought out my friendship. I was a lone walker in the woods, a perfect candidate for a friend. Imps are at heart lonely creatures.

"Hello sir- what's your hurry?"

I laughed. I had to laugh. I was the same way at that age, always eager for companionship. I'm far older now, and little has changed.

He was a red imp, and I felt a certain camaraderie with him. So I decided to indulge him. I'd advise against such trickery, as some young children may throw tantrums that can lead to bad consequences for the tricker.

"I'm not in a hurry, my friend. I just walk quickly. Life is short you know."

The child was small in stature, about the height of a house cat, and watching his little legs speed up to catch up to my gait was priceless. He wore filthy overalls and a hat. I could tell he liked that I called him a friend. He paused for some time. "Not for me, sir. For me, life is very long. I'm already quite older than you, do you know that?"

"Oh I don't know. I'm pretty old myself. How old are you?"

The imp rubbed his chin in thought as he ran at my side. It

was a funny sight. "One hundred and thirty. Eight. 138. How old are you?"

I smirked but I didn't looked back his way. You have to be in control of a friendship with an imp. Or else they walk all over you. "I'm so old I've forgotten my age, young one. I know I don't look it."

"What is your name?"

"My name is Harold. What is yours?"

"My name is Apple-Eater."

"Apple-Eater? Who named you that?" Often, we are named by our human friends.

The imp had an expression of nostalgia and looked off into the heavily wooded distance. It was very amusing to me, watching his little legs move so quickly while his face was so serene. So I sped up.

"My first friend named me Apple-Eater. What a wonderful person. I ran into my friend in the woods, where my parents abandoned me a long, long time ago. See, my mother is a fairy and my father is an imp, and they decided to run off together to the fairy kingdom. And so they left me alone. I thought they'd return, but after fifty years, I decided they probably were not coming back."

Such is the tale for virtually all imps. The father and mother leave Monello and all its people behind, and the child is left to fend for itself. This is one reason few of us ever venture out to find love. The trauma of such a loss of attachment is the imp's first formative experience in the world. No wonder we all seek companionship early on.

"Was he good to you? Your friend, I mean, the one that named you."

"It was a girl. And yes she was very good to me."

I sighed with relief. Females are often better friends than males. Until they grow up.

"Until--" Here it comes.

24

CHAPTER 1

"Un-n-" he began to weep, slowly at first and then freely. I imagined I'd given him more attention than any passers-by had in a long time. Maybe that's why he felt so comfortable with me. Then again he could be working me for some kind of scheme. Or he could be an older imp, like my brother, pretending to be a child, getting in one last hurrah with me. Either way, he was going to stop crying right now.

I didn't slow my walking down and neither did he. I turned to stifle a laugh. He was crying and running at the same time. "She grew older and then fell in love. She had children. While I always wanted to play, she just stopped. She stopped playing and started sweeping, and raising her own children, and cooking. She promised we'd always be friends and play together. She changed."

"The humans change so quickly." Then I caught myself. "We humans change so quickly. You are still a child at 138 years. No humans even live that long. We pass through our seasons in a shadow's breath."

He wiped away tears that certainly looked real. "Alice was her name. She went apple picking and wandered a bit too far from home. I was hiding behind some bushes, watching her, thinking she must be lonely like me, for she was alone. Not all who are alone are lonely, I've learned. I was timid. I approached her, trying to see what she was up to. Was she pulling any tricks, playing any games? She saw me and laughed. Said she never saw someone so small. She thought I was a fairy or an elf. Or something like that."

"I asked if I could help and we made a game out of it. Whoever picked the most apples wins. I won. Part of me feels that Alice let me win. I was not the best picker. We carried them back to her parents' cottage in two big sacks.

"I stayed hidden out of sight per her instructions but I remained watchful as she triumphantly presented the sacks to her mother. Her mother opened one of the sacks and dropped it back to the floor, astonished. 'Alice!' she exclaimed. 'I asked you to go out into the woods and pick apples, not rocks!' She turned over the sack and to Alice's surprise, rocks fell out of all shapes and sizes. 'Go back out and pick apples this time!' her mother demanded, slamming the door.

"I laughed and laughed and so did she. Alice was a good sport then. She asked, 'so what did you do with all the apples? I'm hungry.' I told her I ate them all! So she called me Apple-Eater from then on.

"It was a neat trick I learned some time ago, to switch things. I showed her a mountain of apples behind the cottage which used to be a mound of rocks. Since Alice's mother was expecting her after a couple of hours of fruit picking, we decided to spend that time playing hide-and-seek. That's how we became good friends. Hide-and seek was our favorite. We would always play."

"Until--"

"Until we didn't. I don't want to talk about it any more, if you please, Harold. Now you're my friend, yes? You called me your friend just before."

I had no interest or intention of keeping up the charade of Harold or to be another note of sorrow for this sad singer. I removed my veil and showed him my true face. He stopped and recoiled from me but I grabbed his little arms. "Be strong, Apple-Eater, and hold onto your happy memories. Do not grow cynical or wicked- play your tricks only for love of the sport, and take heart. I am older than you and have seen many winters. But true as I stand before you now, they are followed by springs, summers and autumns." Then I disappeared.

I needed to leave; I couldn't stay and play with Apple-Eater. It would have been a deception to continue the conversation in the guise of interest. The boy needed to learn to trust himself and not force himself on other people. When you are young, you tend to believe the sun revolves around you. When you grow up, you find the harsh truth that you are lucky just to be a witness to the movement of the skies.

I hadn't thought about him again after I reappeared at the next pond, which I knew was close by. I retried my locating spell. Vanna and Warlocke were somewhere east of my location. They were the only beings I knew of who could, and I hoped, would, help me become human.

The sun was setting; it was pushing tree shadows out above me. As the sun was setting west and I was moving east, I decided it was a good time to stop for the night. I climbed up a very large oak tree and rested on a high branch. My kind doesn't sleep usually, unless it is a satisfied Impsleep after pulling a monumental heist or other project. That kind of sleep tends to lend itself to impish dreams. Dreams of future exploits, and happy memories of exploits past.

I wanted to try sleeping and dreaming as the humans do. Every night, not knowing where they go off to. Each morning returning from afar. It must be both frightening and exciting. Perhaps I could induce myself to sleep like a person. I tried to concentrate on the sounds around me. There were hoots from stray owls and the beginning symphony of crickets, soothing me to sleep. I was as they say, out like a light.

I was out, but where did I go? I didn't know for a long time. At first I had only darkened sensations of floating and flying for what felt like four hundred years. Movement in all directions, outward and upward, downward and backward, repeating. Flying and falling, going far away and finally arriving in a dream.

I became vaguely aware that I was riding a horse. It was trotting quickly, but not quite galloping. No- I was not riding the horse, I was driving a carriage pulled by a horse. I had the reins in my hands and we were at a clearing. I was rushing back somewhere. I had to get there as fast as I could, but the horse could only take so much, and pushing it too hard was not a good idea. I went close to whisper to it. "Come on Mayberry, you can--"

SMASH!!! I fell from the tree without finishing the dream. Would you believe it? I got a small taste of it but lost my balance, unused as I was to remaining still while my mind wandered into another realm. This was a skill humans possessed that must be learned. It is a sorcery that magical creatures do not know.

The sun was rising in the east so I walked in that direction, greeted by the ascending, glowing sphere of day. I felt oddly refreshed, and yet yearning to have finished my dream. But I was close to the home of Vanna and Warlocke, I could sense it. So I walked in my usual brisk pace.

I didn't know where the next pond or body of water was, so I walked in faith. If either Vanna's cottage or a pond was not found sometime this morning, then I'd have to backtrack to lower terrain and find water.

I'd first heard of Vanna and Warlocke in my travels. They were both humans who were highly skilled in the magical arts. Vanna was a witch and Warlocke was a wizard. They are what would be considered an older couple, each some 350 years of age. I do believe Vanna is 20 or so years older than him. They fell in love in their youth, when she was 90 and he was 70.

They owned an alchemy shop in their younger days, where they concocted healing elixirs, love potions, and offered astrologic advice. They had a reputation for being very powerful and very just. Their kindness was legendary. They were good people, but also stern.

I'd met them during my time as Harlequin, King Leonard's royal advisor, though I doubt they would recognize me. I sometimes change what "Harold" looks like. They assisted the royal house in healing citizens during a particularly dark time when we'd suffered a small plague. While they helped people in need, I was jockeying in the king's opulent court, convincing him and others to walk about naked. I could not help but feel a morsel of guilt.

My purpose has never been to help anything or anyone. My

purpose has been to indulge myself and do the things that I loved to do. That is the purpose of all naturally magic creatures. Scrunch! I stopped. I was being followed from afar. There was someone or something on my tail, with plenty of cover in which to remain hidden.

I thought I heard something earlier but attributed it to the wind. A calm wood can become agitated by the beat of a butterfly's wings. But make no mistake, I am being stalked by a creature whose intentions I don't know. And yet, my furtive kind has little fear. An imp enjoys reversing this kind of hunt.

So I walked downhill to look for a water source. Slowly. It took me an hour of slow walking to find a stream. It was good enough to make my last attempt at finding the human masters. Instead I decided to lie down and close my eyes, and pretend to sleep. When I heard the rustling of leaves some way yonder, I transported myself to my unsolicited follower.

I appeared behind him. He was moving methodically to be as quiet as possible, but my senses are quite refined. I tapped him on the shoulder and jumped back as he turned quickly around trying to maul me. He growled and lunged, scratching at me. He had long brownish blond hair, a dark beard and silver eyes.

I was quicker than he, however. I dodged each lunge. This only made him angrier. And faster. "Who are you?" He barked. We lunged and dodged to a standstill.

"My name is Harold! Who are you? And why were you following me?" He seemed calmer now. Perhaps he was just startled by my sneaking up behind him.

"My name is Radegast. What do you want with these woods, Harold?"

"What do you mean?"

"There is a witch near here. You are looking for her. Tell me, Imp: What do you want with her?"

I was taken aback. How did he know?

Then I saw it in his silver eyes. He was two-natured. His

second nature was wolf. No wonder he was such a good tracker, and so fast. But how could he know my nature? It's not as if we have a particular smell. I'm proud to say I'm mostly odorless.

He let his guard down, perhaps seeing my confusion and reading my lack of ill intent. So I attempted to lie. "I wish to sell her sugar cookies. I'm a baker from a far-off country who wishes to relocate here."

"Here?" He asked, looking around at the wilderness.

"No, not right here, but the nearest town from here. And that would be...?" I looked in two opposite directions to let him know how lost I was.

"Not really a town, more of a feudal kingdom. Mansfield, and it's that way." He pointed. I began to walk in that direction when he put a hand on my chest. "So let me understand, you're a baker who is moving from a far-away land to a place whose name he doesn't know, and is approaching the house of a powerful witch in order to sell her... sugar cookies. Cookies that, I assume you will bake once you set up shop in Mansfield, whose existence you just discovered now?"

I knew it didn't sound believable, but you would honestly be surprised at how little sense you need to make in order to trick most people. "Yes."

He crossed his arms. He was my height, tall for this part of the wilderness. "And where is the far off land you hail from, traveler Harold? Is it by any chance Monello?"

I was curious, and amused. Most things amused me at my age. A werewolf crossing his arms at me in human form held its own charm. "Why do you ask, Sir Radegast?"

He unfolded those arms and looked forlorn. He turned from me and paused, breathing in the noon air. Then he turned back to me. "Sir Radegast. That used to be my title. I was a knight-Captain of the King's Order, the highest ranking knight in all my kingdom. But I was unhappy with just that. I wanted more, you see. And the ambition felled me like a rotted tree.

CHAPTER 1

"I resolved to woo the princess into marrying me, not out of love, but out of desire to become king. The power of the throne held me in thrall, not her fair face. Once we married I intended to kill her father and thus be crowned ruler of the land. The witch Vanna whom you seek, was the king's advisor and saw through my intentions. Thereafter I was cast out of the kingdom and sentenced to walk the woods in exile. No place to call home."

He went on. "Since my deception was for evil purposes, Vanna cursed me to become a werewolf, a child of two natures. Thus I could never be deceptive again, for should I try, I would instantly transform into a hideous beast. I must wear my true nature on the outside, black, dark, ever hungry. But I was also given the burden of seeing the true nature of others. I see behind the mask that others wear. That is how I know who you are, Er--"

I pointed a fast finger at him, glowing my eyes reddish-gray for effect. "Do NOT say that name aloud! Not in these woods. That name and its possessor are not safe. Please," I softened.

"As you wish. But do not tell me, 'Harold', that you wish to sell cookies to the witch. Your deception will be found out if you lie to me again. Do not make me uneasy. Tell me the truth and I will let you pass."

Let me pass? But the witch cursed him- why would he care if my intentions were noble or ignoble? As dim as I am, I understood then. Radegast became Vanna's protector after the incident that made him werewolf. He is atoning for his sins, challenging his own savage spirit, taming it, mastering it, using it for better purposes. He truly sees the error of his ways. Or he would not be here, folding his arms at me.

"Believe me, Radegast, when I say that I understand you. It is difficult to have a nature you do not want. I wish to change, and become human. I knew Vanna about a hundred years ago, and legend of her greatness has only grown. The truth is that I am tired of my immortal life and prankish spirit. I am going to beg her to turn me human, as you once were."

He looked into my eyes, searing those silver spheres into me. He patted my right shoulder. There was no deception in my speech, and he let me go, even telling me the best way to get to the cottage. Just over the next hill, past the green meadow, a humble shack is her palatial home.

"Tell Vanna that Radegast is still watching over her. And always will. I wish you well in your endeavor, but I warn you: it is not easy to be something you are not. Especially human."

"Thank you." I considered what he said and wondered at his tenacity. Respect is not something common to me, but I suppose I respected him.

Over the next hill were a field of daisies- Vanna's garden, no doubt. This was all her and Warlocke's territory, under the protectorate of Radegast. It was a safe, peaceful haven. I should want to retire here if ever the future allowed it to be so.

So I walked through the field of daisies and saw the cottage. It is not big at all. Palatial, Radegast? It is, as a matter of both fact and opinion, quite tiny. It would be a grand palace for elves or fairies, perhaps. But not for grown humans.

I walked up to the house and steeled myself. I felt something I'd never felt before. I was nervous. And I was experiencing that very human feeling of relying on powers greater than my own. I knocked on the heavy wooden door but it only made the whisper of a sound. So I knocked again. Practically nothing could be heard.

Impatient, I called out, "Excuse me! Is Vanna or Warlocke in today? I have something to ask of them."

I knocked once more, much harder this time. There was very little sound that the door made, even when it opened. "Hello?"

I heard a gravelly female voice as if the speaker were right in front of me. "We don't want any sugar cookies!" she said. And then cackled in all her charm.

She opened up the door. "Hello Vanna," I said. She looked

CHAPTER 1

older. It had been a century since I saw her at Leonard's Court. Those years did not treat her too well nor did she age gracefully. Seeming impressed, I complimented, "You look fantastic."

"And you look like you're lying as usual." With a warm smile she shooed me in.

When I walked into the place it truly was palatial on the inside. It looked like the interior of a fine castle- not dreadfully opulent but by no means poor. "How on earth…" I began.

"Ye are a Master of Deception and yet ye cannot see the deception in others. It is a wondrous paradox. My home is cloaked in magic. Appearances are the only things we know. They are the only we encounter the world…and yet appearances are deceiving. So we can never truly know anything at all."

"Yes, they are," I nodded in perplexed agreement. I noticed she'd made some honey golden tea and a cup was already waiting for me on the table. Honey golden tea, not golden honey tea. Vanna was very adamant that I know the difference. One was made from honey and the other was made from gold. It was both hot and aromatic. There was cinnamon and bergamot.

Vanna's accent had always made me laugh because it would usually change to fit the situation. I didn't know her true tongue or her true dialect. A hundred years ago, it was different.

I sat at the table. At least I tried to. "Ouch! Get off of me!" I heard the chair say. It was Warlocke, who must have been comfortably seated at the chair I wanted, however he was invisible.

Vanna laughed at me again. She was right, though. How strange that I can make illusions and turn invisible myself, and yet I cannot see through the illusions of others. If I can be so easily fooled, then I assume everyone can.

Warlocke materialized into his seat. They were both an old, wilting pair. Vanna had a deep pallor, haggardly disheveled hair, and a cloudy film over her pale blue eyes. Warlocke did not fare much better. He also had white hair, which was long and greasy, and a long white beard. They both wore what looked like gray rags as clothing. And their teeth were yellow- that is, the few teeth they still possessed were yellow.

I did not know Vanna well, and she hardly knew me when we were both living in the same kingdom. Both of us were useful to the king at different times of his life. It is a good thing people these days are tolerant of witches and witchcraft, something I'm sure will never change.

She motioned me to have a seat across from her and Warlocke, and to have some tea. I thanked her, and had a sip. It was delicious.

I wanted to wait for some kind of introduction, but they both simply looked at me and stared politely. Vanna had more interest in me than Warlocke did, who had now lit up a thin pipe, into which he placed the sweetest-smelling tobacco ever to grace my very old nostrils.

I decided to begin. "Vanna, I come to you begging for your vast gifts, to bestow upon me a hex."

She smiled and her eyes sparkled. She was beautiful centuries ago. "A hex, sayeth the Lord of the Imps?" I looked nervously at Warlocke. He simply puffed away at his pipe, his eyes seeming to be resting somewhere far, possibly the dark of the moon from the looks of it.

"It is not safe for me that others know who I am or what I'm doing," I instructed her, pointing to Warlocke with my head. She shook her head in an understanding and contemplative way. Tsk tsk.

Her eyes lit up brilliantly as if in the throes of a portentous prophecy. "For ye to seek out my aid, King Erubaca, thou must comprehend how grave thy decision truly is. It must be this way, you see. For only among friends can ye ask of so great a thing. I know what ye come here for but not why." I offered nothing, but then again, she had asked nothing.

"It doesn't matter why ye come. Thou ask a great deed be done, and the price must also be great."

CHAPTER 1

Let me explain just some minor things before I continue. I am actually the imp king Erubaca. Yes, that's right, Erubaca. My true name. You have perhaps heard of me. The Northeners know me as Loki. Those of this Bohemian region know me as Rumpelstiltskin. There are legends and myths about me that traverse far and wide. The reason I fear the knowledge of others is that my position is dangerous. Should others know me, the fate of my kind would be in their hands. Such is the same with elves, faeries, dwarves, and most other magical creatures.

There exists a Council of Magic Royalty, where the heads of all the magic creatures meet and discuss ways to maintain peace among one another. In attendance is the Queen Pixie, King Elf, Lady Faerie, Lord Dwarf, myself and many others. We tell no one of this council, so long as we are members. For if we become found out, the fate of our kingdoms would be in peril by the greed of others, who might seek to overthrow us. Doing so would unhinge our very delicate peace.

So you see, the fact that Vanna and Warlocke knew of my position as king, and also my name, could have put all imps at risk if their intentions were anything but noble. I doubted for only a moment, then it passed.

Fortunately the witch and the wizard were kind and gentle souls, who I believe have recently become two trees in the forest, and whose spirits guide lost travelers on their way. Since this story of mine is already nearly a century old, you see, they have passed on since then.

"I have much gold," I told her. Collecting gold from unsuspecting victims for hundreds of years can come in quite handy. "Fifty pounds of king's gold, the purest there is." I reached into my satchel and pulled out a coin to show her. It had the face of King Leonard on it.

She held it in her hand, weighing it, unimpressed. "To be honest, Lord Erubaca, it would have been better to have fifty pounds of silver, or even iron, since gold is hardly ever an ingredient in one of my brews. Except for honey golden tea, that is. Silver and iron have much more magical potency. They both inhibit magical effects and so are perfect materials for defensive spells."

I nodded. I should have known. Though I didn't wield the same kind of magic as a witch or a wizard, I should have known what would pass off best as currency would have been something of magical value.

"I can go out into town, into Mansfield, which I hear is close by and trade my gold for silver. The humans would be happy to trade with me. Then I can pay you my debt."

Vanna scratched her hairy, warty chin that only Warlocke could love. "Yes, well I suppose that could work. Except I certainly do have quite enough silver and iron. I never run out, ye see, of anything. I'm fully stocked for the next century. My concoctions don't require fifty pounds of any single ingredient." She made a gulping sound, and continued staring at me, nodding her head maternally. She reached out and patted my hand.

So, then, how was I to pay? "So how, then, Vanna, am I to pay? My gold, and anything it can buy, is apparently no good to you."

She smiled that beautiful ancient smile again, flashing rotted teeth and withered wrinkles. "Why, thy ring of course. It is one of the most enchanted objects in the forest."

I looked down at my hand with unease. My ring is what is called in magic terms a "binding talisman." It's what the sorcerer in Arabia used to make me serve him as genie. Its owner is bound to it. And by it. Through magic or witchcraft, the wielder of the ring is in control of its true possessor- me. Through me, they may rule my people.

The ring is the source of all the magic imps possess. Not only does the possessor have the "keys to the kingdom," so to speak. They have the kingdom itself. So long as they are versed in the magical arts, they can use the ring to take over Imp Magic completely and entirely, and therefore all of Monello. And so you see why it is that I dread telling anyone with powers about who I am. I can tell you all, since you are human.

I began to protest but Vanna interrupted. "Now understand this, Erubaca, if ye are going to be human, ye cannot possess yer talisman. It's dangerous and ye can't protect yerself, or it, as ye can now. Trust us. If ye didn't, then ye shouldn't have come. If we'd wanted all the gold and magic in the world, we'd have had it by now. But as it is, we have spent our lives in the service business, helping others. Yer ring is safest with us."

Warlocke puffed out a cloud of fragrant smoke. "Too right, too right."

I believed them both. It's not because I'm good at picking apart truth from lie- I'm not. I could be easily tricked by someone clever enough. I'm not the best reader of intentions but I have gotten better. My feelings were correct, however. Those two were very good people. They proved it often. And it was also correct to say that their power was already far greater than mine, so the item to be handed over meant little to them, except to watch over it. "Okay. You are right." I gave them my ring, and they put it away in a locked room with what I imagine to be all their other rare possessions.

"I must tell ye, Erubaca, that I cannot change who ye are, only what ye are. Yer heart, the very center of yer self, will be the same. That is something only ye can change should ye wish to."

I considered her sentiment and reflected how Erumite had told me basically the same thing. I told her, "Humans have the greatest capacity for change that I have ever seen. They are the only creatures that even try to change. I will be happy as one of them."

Vanna chuckled heartily and even Warlocke cracked open a sliver of a smile, through which sweet smoke poured out. She rebutted, "I've been human some three hundred odd years, my friend. Happy is something I haven't been very often. But those few moments are precious and we live for them." She put her hand on my forearm, consolingly.

Such a transformation would surely be traumatic. Forgetting her predilection for clairvoyance, I began to speak. But before I could let out a sound, she said, "Don't worry, it will not hurt."

"Have you ever done this kind of thing before?" I asked nervously, drinking more of the starkly flavored tea.

"Transforming one creature into another? Yes, I have. It always happens at a high cost, however. For ye it is yer crown, yer power, yer immortality. Yer very self, perhaps."

I wrung out my hands. "Will I remember anything? What will the transformation be like?"

"Well, ye already look human. Ye'll look more-or-less like this after the transformation is complete, and I assume ye will go by 'Harold' in all future endeavors. Ye may have a spot of forgetfulness, a sense of amnesia about the past, but that fogginess will lift after some time. From what I can reckon, yer kind should be able to handle the change. Other creatures I have made this spell for, never remember."

I looked over to her far wall. I could see some kind of calendar with strange writing and markings. Maybe it was an astrological calendar. "Today is Midsummer's Eve," she said. "An important day for witches and witchcraft alike."

I nodded and took a deep breath. "I'm ready, Vanna. Let us begin. But before we start, I want to thank you from the bottom of my foolish heart."

She smiled kindly. "You're welcome. But we've already begun. Your tea. It's more potent than it tastes. There's not just honey and gold in it- there's also enchanted silver, raven's quill and a few other choice ingredients."

Of course there was. I'd always said the trick is easiest played on the tricker. Well done, Vanna. At least now I couldn't back out. I thought silver was only anti-magic, but apparently it could be enchanted. After she'd told me what was in my tea, I began to feel things I'd never felt. I assumed it's what people felt like when they were sick, since I'd seen and observed such human nuances, but of course never got sick myself.

My palms were sweaty and I was hot with fever. Yet I felt chilled and shook uncontrollably. I began to cough, which I'd never done before- it was not a pleasant new experience. Vanna went in the other room to grab a blanket and drape it over me. "Ye need to make yer way over to that bed there, where ye'll sleep it off."

I tried to do as she asked but I could hardly move at this point. The elixir worked quickly, like a poison, but differently. Though I'd felt awful, I had an undercurrent of the potion working its way through me. I could feel it working, even though I was in the throes of something like a great illness.

The next few minutes were very unclear to me as I began to lose my senses. There was noise and shuffling, and I do believe Warlocke aided Vanna in carrying me over to the bed. I felt sorry for them both, being of so advanced an age and yet having to perform manual labor. I'm heavier than I look. Another deception.

I was comfortable in my bed and about to go completely under when Vanna shook me into some semblance of sense. "Now it's very important that I tell ye this, Harold. When ye awaken, ye will be human. But there is a caveat to this spell. If ye should act impish- play a trick, pull a scam, do anything devious- ye will return to yer former self as soon as the trick is complete. For some time ye will forget all else, but this ye will remember: bear not mischief. It becomes thee not."

I could not reply; I fell right into oblivion. I wanted to tell her, "Radegast still watches over you" but all the lights dimmed and I traveled far beyond the borders of my mind and body. I returned to the dream I was having in the forest, back to the carriage I was driving earlier.

A great fear gripped me, was all around me. I needed to hur-

ry but the poor horse was exhausted. My Mayberry. The need
to pass the clearing and be at my destination was overwhelming.
Though I was present in that moment, I did not know where I
was going or why I had to get there so quickly. I felt a rising
paranoia needling me and pushing me forward. But no matter
how fast I was going, it was not fast enough.

The horse, which was a pale gray color with pale red eyes,
began to stumble. No, no, NO! We could not stop here, we were
right out in the open. The grass was low in this clearing, without any trees or bushes for cover. Animals in the forest clip the
blades of grass as they eat, and so it remains short here.

I thought about climbing down and running for the woods,
but again, a paralysis swept over me. I could not leave the car-
riage- I must continue to bring the cargo I carry to the place
where I am going. But where is that? What is the cargo? Who
am I? The confusion was just as deep as my panic.

Like a rush of wind, another carriage ran up to me. It had
three riders in red hooded robes. No- this is what I feared most,
to be discovered by others as I passed through. To be impeded
without getting to my destination. I'd pulled the reins of my
carriage to a stop. "Ho there. Would your name be Harold,
perchance? We seek Harold for recompense." He stopped and
gazed over me, his face obscured by darkness. "Yes, you are he."

I could not see the speaker but heard his gruff voice bellowing out from under his hood. The three of them approached me
with their heads bent low. One of them reached out their right
hand, palm up. The hand was withered and old. It trembled
with advanced age. "You owe us for the evils you've committed
against us. Give us payment."

This small gesture was incredibly frightening. I didn't know
what these people wanted from me, or what I possibly could
have owed them. The unshakeable sense that I did indeed harm
them in some way, that I owed them for it, resounded within me.
"Give us payment." they said in unison. "You owe us."

CHAPTER 1

Without a question, I checked my own person for any stray coins. I had a satchel. I looked within it but found nothing. It was empty. "What can I possibly give you? I haven't anything to give."

"You do have something," the first speaker said. Slowly he pointed to the carriage. "Give us your cargo."

All I could think of was that this was wrong. And yet, I did owe them. I wanted to rectify my debt but did not want to lose my cargo. I looked up at them, my own head bent low, hands in a prayer. "Is there no other way?"

They said in unison, "No."

They boarded nimbly and we all went to the back of the carriage. There was a simple wooden casket there. A casket for a body. It surprised me as much as it delighted them. "Give us the coffin." I could not give it up. It was special. It was holy. But for my life, I did not know what it was.

"Who are you?" I began to cry. I'd never cried before but it felt wholly natural.

"We are humanity," they said. "And you owe us. For a thousand years of treachery."

The first two took off their hoods to reveal Vanna and Warlocke. The third did not doff his or her hood. "Give us the body, Harold," Vanna said.

"N-n-no, please. Anything else."

"This is the price you must pay, Harold."

"I-I'm afraid. I'm lost! Can't you see how lost I am?"

"Give us the body, Harold," the third, still-hooded member of their trio said. His voice was like frozen snow.

I could not stand it any longer. I abandoned my cargo. "Fine! Take it! Take the body yourselves! I won't help you carry it."

They descended upon the casket like vultures on a carcass. In a way, that's exactly what they were. They removed the cover of the unassuming wooden coffin. Inside was a red body head to toe. Inside was Erubaca.

I screamed.

CHAPTER 2

I awoke in early autumn or late summer. In either event it was September. I knew it was September because there was a briskness in the air and the leaves were delicate contrasts of orange, yellow and brown. I'd never taken the time to look at the leaves before, or appreciate their inherent beauty. Not that I recalled. I took a deep breath, and allowed the odor of pine and chestnut to fill my nostrils.

It was a new awakening in so many ways. I woke up on a pile of leaves in the middle of the woods. Confused, achy, head throbbing, eyes pounding, I felt happy to be alive. The day was beautiful and the wind carried the inhalation and exhalation of the world with it. For a moment, I decided to let it flow through me with my eyes closed.

When I opened them again, I noticed I was very hungry. I had pangs of yearning for food. I didn't remember ever feeling such things. Then again, at the time, I didn't remember anything at all, let alone my own name. Who and what I was...that would have to wait to be answered. I needed to eat.

Harvests happen in the fall. The fall is the season when the spring's hard work is collected. The very earth becomes ready to be reaped. I sought out anything that looked edible.

I picked chestnuts, berries, and tarot root which I found near a tall tree. They were delicious and filling. I thought how the root could be made into a hearty tea, and how the berries would be perfect for a pie. For the first time I gathered inspiration from the world, with which to create. I had ideas whose source I did not know but I was thankful for the help.

The next idea to come to me was the idea to find a safe haven. I didn't know what existed in the leaf covered clearing in which I awoke, but there appeared to be nothing there for me. Now that I nourished my body, I began to crave human contact. I was far away from home...or was I? Where was it that I belonged? Loneliness is a terrible new feeling- why did I never remember feeling it before?

I began walking down a poorly-made path. It was barely there, but a path it was nevertheless. I reasoned that if someone made the path no matter how poorly, then it must lead to somewhere. Nothing leads to nowhere- right?

So I followed it, collecting nuts from trees as I walked. There were some plants still flowering, some with white or red buds, some with yellow bulbs, and there were herbs which I thought to myself could be used in cooking and medicine. I put the edibles into the satchel that I had with me when I awoke. I walked past a particular herb which, for some reason, gave me fright. There was something about it I did not like.

The path eventually lead to a walkway parallel to a stream. Or a brook- I didn't know the difference between them, or how I knew anything at all. I didn't recall receiving any kind of formal education. But then again, I also forgot how I learned what a school even was. That day was my first day. I supposed that my amnesia should have caused me fear, but it did not. My heart felt light as a hen's feather, though I didn't remember how it was that I knew anything about feathers or hearts or hens.

I dropped the satchel I had with me, which contains the jewels I picked from the Earth. Indeed, the world provides in the greatest and least of ways. It both enables our lives and restricts them. Looking at the satchel gave me the vague recollection of a familiar dream...but I suppressed my thoughts before I allowed myself to reunite with the memory of that dream. I had to move on, could not remain in one place so far from others. I had to discover where it was that I belonged.

The water in the brook-stream was clear. You could see every smooth stone at the bottom, which was not very far down. The stream was not so deep. I peered over and looked closely and what I saw astounded me. Hello there, me. I saw my reflection, the reflection of a handsome bearded stranger.

Today was like being born a man without having ever been a child. In many ways I did not know at the time, that was precisely right. I'd had a beard and curly black hair. I looked good, and I was happy about that. Not happy- proud. I both liked and disliked the feeling. I later learned that pride was both a love and a hatred of oneself.

I washed my handsome face in the water, took a good deep drink, and moved on. I was reinvigorated. I could feel I was approaching something, somewhere, important.

Roughly half a kilometer past the stream I reached a large town. Or a small city. Or a fiefdom. I did not know what it was when I arrived, but what I did know was that I'd reached civilization. A place where other people lived. A living space that hopefully I, too, could join. If I could not fathom my past life, then I should work towards building a new one. There was no sense in the present going to waste. All I wished for was to belong with others like me.

The sign at the gate said "Welcome to Mansfield. Humans only beyond this point". I smiled when I read that, because I realized I was literate. "I could be the town doctor!" I whispered to myself in elation.

There was a large fortified wall surrounding the entire city.

As I approached the heavy double wooden doors at the front gate, I saw archers from high towers above point their bows at me. "Halt! Who goes there?" a voice from within the compound yelled. "Be ye man or something else?"

Bewildered, I responded, "Um. Man." I think. I pinched myself and it hurt.

"What business have ye with Mansfield?"

That question was much easier to answer. To have somewhere in which to belong, of course. Mansfield is better than a lonely forest. "I wish to settle and make a life for myself here."

"Ye seek immigration? Have ye any skills? Know ye any trades?"

"I am a baker." I paused. "And I am literate."

I could hear an audible gasp from behind the gates and whispers among several people.

"And do ye come with pure intentions to this honest place? Do you wish to add to the kingdom rather than take from it?"

"This more than anything, sir."

"Then traveler, ye are welcome to make a home here in Mansfield upon one very strict condition. Ye must understand, this place is a crossroads of many creatures and much magic. Mansfield has been attacked on more than one occasion by non-humans. We can't let in every person that simply looks human, as ye seem to be.

"Some creatures may be disguised as people but are really something else. We have dogs that will sniff ye to verify yer humanity. If ye be human, ye may stay. If not, those trueshot archers up there will release their arrows into yer spleen. Understand?"

Afraid but trusting, I nodded. There was no reply. Then I realized the voice couldn't see me since it was behind the great doors. Silly oaf, I thought to myself. "Yes, I understand, sir." I did not like to rely on powers greater than my own- and yet I had no choice. As a human, you are not only at the mercy of the elements, but of one another as well.

The immense doors slowly opened to me. A large dog on a leash calmly walked up to me and sniffed. What do magical creatures smell like? I wondered. Perhaps a hint of cinnamon. I then thought of a wonderful new dessert I could make with cinnamon. The dog walked back through the doors. I felt some relief. Then those doors closed again for some reason. My sense of relief changed to terror.

I looked up at the archers and saw that they were standing down. Their bows were no longer trained on me. Relief returned. The doors opened again more fully and I walked through them, a new citizen of Mansfield. Or so I thought.

The gentleman whom I thought of as "the voice" a minute earlier wound up being an elderly man in a blue robe. It looked like a very ceremonial vestment. Blue was the official color of Mansfield, I discovered later. He had thick white sideburns and hooked nose, along with one or two sharp teeth. The man, who introduced himself to me as "Al", had a very outgoing and pleasant demeanor.

"So, ye're a baker who can read, are ye? We can use one of those I admit. I'm the town Gatekeeper and scribe." He smiled and winked at me. "I can read too." I felt a small bit of kindred pride, but that may have been his.

Al grabbed a parchment that was nearby on a writing desk and took a feather quill from an ink well. "Now then, state yer name and age."

What was my name? I thought that if there were any memories buried deep in my mind, I should quickly let them out if at all possible. I stuttered. "Harold. And...twenty...seven. Yes, twenty-seven."

"Harold what? What's yer surname, sir? Heh. Did ye like my joke, fella?"

"Yes, very much. Call me Harold Baker."

"Alright, Harold Baker it is, young sir. Now, another matter, very important. Do ye have any silver er gold of yer own? If ye do, ye may purchase property right now and we'll set ye up with a place. If ye don't, ye may earn yer keep by being put in the royal castle in the service of the royal family. Perhaps King Sabrian might employ ye to read to him, along with proffering baked goods."

I didn't know whether I brought anything with me. I simply awoke in the forest and began walking, some inner desire driving me forward. I opened my satchel and perused what exactly was in there. There was a crust of moldy bread, which thoroughly disgusted me. There was a wineskin flask which, upon closer inspection showed that it had turned to vinegar. There were the foodstuffs that I'd packed, but few of those were left thanks to my selfish stomach.

There was also a glass jar. Within the jar were five silver pieces. I picked it up and showed it to Al. "This is all I have."

He looked at it and nodded. "A worthy start, young lad. Ye will have more than five soon enough. But ye can't afford property just quite yet, so I must put you in residence at the castle. The King is a fine ruler, lad. Ye needn't worry."

"Here." I handed him the jar of silver. "Take it, it's yours now. What I make of myself from this point on is not what I brought with me. It's what I earn. Everything old is gone, now is my new life. Enjoy it, Sir Al. You can always pay me back by purchasing my tea biscuits. I plan on using cinnamon and sugar to make them."

He looked me over with furrowed brows. "Ye're very true-hearted, Mr. Baker. I thank ye very much. But I can't--"

I rose my hand to stop any further argument. "You can. Consider it an act of good faith. My first act as a citizen."

Al laughed merrily. "Well, me kind lad, yer not a citizen yet. It takes a little bit of time. But ye know what? I'll help ye along, how's that sound? I'll get ye made official yet." He motioned to the entire enclosed kingdom, which was quite large once you got inside. "Go explore yer new country for a few hours and then come back. I'll get a guard to show ye to the servant's quarters in the castle once ye return."

I thanked him and then turned to the beautiful town kingdom. The road from the gate led to a large main square with many merchants selling their wares within. It was a thriving marketplace. A fountain was in the middle of the square and it was decorated with gorgeous mermaid-like sculptures. I could see that the wall around the kingdom went all the way around it. The kingdom and therefore the wall was much bigger than it first appeared.

The layout of Mansfield was this- it was basically a large circle. The main entrance, which is the set of wooden doors that I walked through to enter, is at the southern tip. Walking north from there is a road that leads to the main square. On the road to the square are houses, apartments and a few smithies.

At the square itself are shops and sellers of all kinds. North of there is a road that leads to the king's main garden. To the furthest east and furthest west were what was known as the king's forest- woods that belonged to the king. In the East Woods there was a small lake and through the West Woods there ran a large creek.

At the center of the kingdom past the garden was the castle of King Sabrian. It was immense and looked like a sturdy stronghold. Blue-tipped spires formed a very attractive facade. Northward beyond the castle, there was a deep valley followed by a hill at the northernmost tip of Mansfield. On the hill was a lookout tower.

Spread throughout the valley and on the hill were some small cottages. I thought to myself that I would much like to live in one of those cottages once I earned enough silver. I would prefer the calmness and serenity of the valley or the hill compared to the hustle and bustle of the center near the square.

This place had everything it needed to maintain itself. Free-flowing water, woods in which to hunt, a garden in which to grow food, sellers and merchants to provide every need of the day. There was also a large silo of grain near the castle in case of a bad harvest.

This place was a dream kingdom. If I lived in the valley I'm sure I would be able to grow tomatoes, potatoes, tarot roots and other root plants, herbs, spices, berries, apples. Anything and everything I could. It would be wonderful if I didn't have to live there alone, I thought. Maybe love is possible- maybe anything is possible, since it hasn't yet come to pass.

I sighed happily. I began walking my way back and happened upon an ale house. It was named The Blue Widower. It was made of heavy logs and looked like a cabin. I didn't remember ever entering an ale house or a pub, so I was happy to have the experience.

When I went in, I saw some dusty tables and stools gathered around them. A few drunk patrons were drinking their cares away at the main bar. These were workers returning from long days of labor. Some didn't work, but then, they didn't have to work. All they needed was the quarter pence necessary to purchase a pint of ale.

I sat down at a table with two men. One had a red beard and long red hair, and the other had dark, shorter hair. "Hello gentlemen," I greeted. "Would you mind terribly if I sat with you both?"

The dark haired one shook his head, "Not at all, have a seat."

The red haired one interrupted his friend and said, "Yes we would mind. We was havin' a private conversation, you know?"

I arose. "Sorry, I didn't mean to interrupt. It's just that I'm new here in Mansfield and was hoping to meet new people. I wanted to just kick back a drink."

The red haired one spat when he talked. "I'll conversate with ya if ye pay fer a round. Ye got money for a round, do ya?"

No, I hadn't. I'd given away my life savings to Al just a few hours earlier. But to be fair, it was a life I didn't remember at the time anyway. Who knows how I came to have the silver that I did? Perhaps I was a despicable robber who stole the money by force. Maybe my forgetfulness was a chance at redemption. I felt good about having gotten rid of the money. A fresh start is the best start.

"Well, I did, but I don't have money right now. If you'd cover me, I will pay you back. I'm going to be a servant of the king, so I'm good for it. By the way, would you know how much servants of the king are paid? We didn't discuss specifics when I spoke to the Gatekeeper earlier."

The redhead blurted out a laugh. I didn't know at what. The darkhead seemed to be a better soul. "I used to be a servant of the king for a couple of years. The pay was a copper piece per week."

I nodded. "I see, I see. And how many copper pieces make a silver piece?"

"Ten."

TEN! Ten copper pieces make a silver piece and the pay is one copper piece per week. That means it would take an entire year to earn five silver pieces. I'd given Gatekeeper Al an entire year's wages! Oh well. I tried to stifle my surprise. "Well thank you for letting me know. And again, my apologies for seating myself at your table without asking." As I went to get up, I noticed that the redhead also arose and began stumbling towards the back of the pub.

"Do you want me to walk you home?" his dark haired friend asked, amicably.

"No, no, no, let me just walk around a couple of times and come on back. That's a full pint I have left. I need to finish that and then go home."

"All right," his friend said. Then to me in a whisper, "I'd better make sure he doesn't fall. Excuse me."

While they were away from the table, a pub maid walked by

and asked me whether I'd wanted to order anything. She was also red-haired, with green eyes and wearing a server's frock. A fiendish feeling rose up inside me. There were so many possibilities. I could order several more pints of ale and then exit before the two men returned, leaving them with the tab.

I could ask the maid for salt, or peppercorns, and put it in the redhead's pint. Then watch from afar as he spits out the horrid aftertaste. I could ask for honey, and use it like glue to stick the redhead's pint to the table. When he tries to pick up the beer bug, it would be difficult to lift, so he would spill the drink all over himself.

All these pranks would be hilarious, I concluded. But something else within me was very powerful- a warning arising from some dark crevice. "It becomes you not," an assertive voice said. I decided to let the prank go. "No, thank you miss. I'm just leaving." The redhead began singing a drunken chant at the other side of the pub. Others hardly seemed to notice as they kept to themselves. Humanity can be so lonely sometimes, even in company. I left them to their business.

After almost eight hours of exploration, I returned to the main entrance. Al was still there, sitting on a stool, waiting for anyone who approaches. Soldiers sat and lounged along with him, waiting for something, anything, to happen.

It must have been, by my reckoning, five in the afternoon. "Hello there, Sir Al."

Al looked at me with suspicious eyes. "Who goes there? I haven't been called 'Sir' since my time in the knighthood. King Sabrian himself knighted me when he was still a boy."

"It's me, Harold. Harold Baker."

He thought it over, scratching his chin. "Ah yes, Harold Baker- the baker who could read! I could read too, ye know. But not so well any more. Ye'll have to forgive my eyes, my old age has got the best of them. Forty-three years old, ye know." He beat his chest to show his ancient vigor. Then he coughed.

I laughed. I liked Al. "Can I go to the servant's quarters in the castle now? You'd told me a soldier would lead me there once I was ready. I'm ready to go."

Al nodded in thought. "Well I would, of course, it's just that King Sabrian and a group of his warriors are about to return. We must stay on our guard until they arrive. We shan't move from our posts 'til we receive 'em. The ones that come back, that is."

It was my turn to nod in thought. "I see. I'll wait of course. But tell me, Sir Al, what are King Sabrian and his warriors returning from?"

He practically beamed with pride. It was very nearly visible. And blinding, at that. "Grand Ogre Hunt. They have them every so often. We were attacked about a month back by a band of ogres that were after our grain. We were able to fight them off and rebuilt the part of the wall that they broke down. Some time later, from our lookout tower we saw a band of ogres close by once again, so we sent a team of warriors to hunt them down."

The lookout tower was at the northern end, and this entrance to which the warriors were returning was at the southern end. How could the person at the north lookout tower be able to see ogres to the south of Mansfield?

"Did the telescope get invented yet?" I asked Al.

"Nay, I don't think so, young Baker."

"Then how could they be sure it was the same group of ogres? Or that this particular band had any bad intentions? Couldn't they have just been passing by?" I didn't know why I was curious or why it had bothered me that my new king leads Ogre Hunts on occasion.

"Well ogres are all driven by their hunger, ye see? Like vampires or nymphs. For them, the easiest meal is best. They see us here, we who work our land, hunt our own forests, and they think we're easy pickins. And to them, the walls that we build are like glass. They plow right through them causing all manner of havoc and mayhem. All ogres are like that, it's their nature.

Oh sure, a few might have good souls or what have ye, but their bellies always win in the end, y'see what I'm saying, Mr. Baker?"

I did, only too well. "Yes, I suppose I do, Sir Al. Why does the king go with them?"

Al smiled a sad smile. "To Lord Sabrian it is a very personal thing to protect his land." He peered through a peep-hole in the wooden door. Then he looked up and I noticed that they had another lookout tower right at the entrance. I hadn't registered it before. That must have been how they'd seen the ogres near the southern border. A soldier looked down to Al and shook his head. No one coming yet.

"Alright, Mr. Baker, we've got a little bit of time. Pull yerself up a stool and sit a spell. I'll swiftly recount to ye the sad tale of our beloved king.

"There was once a lasting peace in Mansfield between humans and non-humans. We're in a very busy location- there are magical creatures that live in the woods just outside of here. Through Sabrian's father, we made treaties with all the other creatures that were nearby. They had safe passage in Mansfield and considered it a haven. A refuge. They'd come and go as they pleased so long as they caused no trouble.

"Then when Sabrian took the throne at the ripe age of 17, things began to change. I think things usually begin to change the very moment they stay the same. Other creatures did not fear or respect him as they did his father. Though he allowed them passage and catered to their needs, some did not appreciate it like they should have. And they underestimated Sabrian.

"They'd learned that his royal archives possessed many magical artifacts, including spellbooks and potions. They became greedy and resolved to conspire against the kingdom to retrieve the artifacts they believed rightly belonged to them. They waited patiently for the perfect time to attack, all the while laughing with us, eating with us, befriending us. Pretending.

"Six years after Sabrian came to power, he'd had a beautiful queen named Ophelia and a young daughter named Syla. They also adopted another daughter named Hyacinth. It was then, on the eve of the seventh anniversary of his coronation, that a small but powerful group of creatures attacked us during a nighttime raid. I was still a knight back then so I saw the battle with me own eyes. Me eyes worked back then.

"A group of Blue Elves and Dark Fairies, along with ogres and dragons they'd summoned, mounted a heavy attack that lasted into the morning. In those days, Mansfield had a witch named Vanna and a wizard named Warlocke in its service. They proved themselves friends of the crown, and if it weren't for them the battle, nay, the entire kingdom would have been lost.

"They pushed back the Blue Elves and the Dark Fairies through some very powerful witchcraft. Sabrian's knights, me among them, along with Sabrian himself, fought off the magic-less ogres and dragons. About when the sun was beginning to rise, the leader of the Blue Elves vanished from the battlefield. He reappeared outside the royal archives. Although the library was enchanted, the Elf was able to open the door. He was about to enter when Ophelia, valiant queen that she was, confronted him.

Al got animated. His tale-telling was very excitable. "Ophelia was well versed in hand-to-hand combat. She also possessed The Clamoring Blade, a sword that always struck true and possessed other potent magic. Syla was young and also nearby, and you know how strong a mother's instincts to protect her young are.

"I won't get into the sad details of that fight, but in the end they slew each other in battle at the foot of the archives. That day, Sabrian lost his wife, his queen, his love. And very nearly his daughter. He forever swore that this breach of trust should not happen again.

No magic creatures, or even humans capable of wielding magic, were allowed passage, or residence any longer. Everyone was expelled. We got no healers, no soothsayers, no alchemists, nothing. He exiled Vanna and Warlocke, with his apologies. They understood his sentiments, and cast an enchantment of protection over the kingdom as they left. And now, here we are, so many years later, seeking to maintain that delicate peace."

It certainly was a lot of honest and tragic information. I spoke in a soft whisper, head bowed low. "Yes, Sir Al, here we are. I am sorry for questioning the king."

"And on yer very first day, Mr. Baker," Al laughed. "In case ye were wondering, the death of his wife was the reason fer making blue the official color of Mansfield. There's lots of reasons to do blue. Blue is the color of inconsolable sadness. Blue was the queen's favorite color. The color of 'er eyes. Blue was the color of the Elf that slew her. If ye don't remember those things that give ye inspiration, then ye lose the inspiration, am I right? Yes. So that's why. Everywhere a reminder."

Above us in the lookout tower, a loud yell of "Hunting party arriving! A kilometer away!" boomed out.

"How many?" screeched Al back at the tower.

"All of them."

I eagerly awaited their arrival. I was far more intrigued with the king now that I heard his story. What good warriors he must also have with him, to boldly go in search of dangerous ogres on their territory.

"How many?" I asked Al.

"All of them," he replied.

"Yes, but how many are in the hunting party?"

"Six. Four volunteers, the king, and his daughter Syla."

Six! Six only. Against at least four powerful, gigantic monsters. How is it they all returned? How is it any of them returned? The physical capacity for destruction, the enduring prowess of ogres, is legendary in any land.

Al commanded four soldiers to open the doors. The six warriors walked in without any pomp, no heralds with trumpets, no marching drums, no ceremony whatsoever. They did not enter in any particular order or while marching to a particular beat. They just, walked in.

There was the king, who was easily markable. He had a silver crown, with some light body armor. His shield was blue, as was his...cape. I supposed it was a cape. The hilt of his sword was also blue. He had short straight hair and dark, intense blue eyes

There were four other men, two of which were knights. I could tell they were knights because of their chain armor, and they wore helmets and ornate shields. There was the crest of Mansfield on them- a golden hawk against a field of blue. The two other men did not wear armor, and in fact, were very dirty. They had grimy faces. They were large men, with swords and shields, and also carried sharpened spears at their sides.

There was also one woman. It must have been Syla. Her hair was as dark as King Sabrian's and her eyes were just as intense. Her armor was blue and the only normal aspect of her get-up was a blue flower in her hair. I wondered to myself how she fought ogres with a flower in her hair, but then decided she must have put it there on the march back to Mansfield.

Gatekeeper Al bowed in reverence to the lot of them. "Welcome King Sabrian and Princess Syla, back from yer noble quest. And Sir Knights, and loyal servants. We eagerly awaited yer return. We've gathered some horses for ye to head back to the palace in haste, get yerselfs cleaned up for the Hunt Parade later tonight." He turned to me. "That's a grand festival we throw every time our warriors return from missions in one piece."

I also bowed to the returning party, along with the soldiers at the gate. The king cast his gaze upon me. Then turned to his trusted gatekeeper. "Who is this man?" He had a gruff, husky voice, heavy with much sorrow. There was also a note of wisdom there.

Gatekeeper Al replied quite animatedly in his way, "Oh why this is Mister Harold Baker, my lord, soon to be a new citizen of the realm. He is to be a new royal servant in your charge. He's a baker AND he can read!"

The king smirked good-naturedly. "He could be the town doctor. I'll tell you what, Harold. Follow us on foot to the castle. While we tidy up and get ready for tonight's festival, you have free reign of my entire kitchen and its staff the rest of the evening. My staff will be fully available to you. I want you to bake with all your skill for the event. It begins promptly at ten o'clock."

I felt honored and also proud that the king of my new country had given me an opportunity to prove myself. I was confident I could excel, and yet, I hadn't truly known at that point whether I could even bake. I only sensed that I could.

The group all got on horseback and rode off to the castle together. Each horse was white with a blue saddle and reins. That made me curious. "Sir Al," I began. "Why didn't they go on their hunt with the horses? Wouldn't that have made it easier for them to come and go?"

"Oh no, Mister Baker. Ogres love horsemeat, everyone knows that. Too dangerous for their mounts, especially at night." I hadn't thought of that. It made sense. I thanked him for all he'd done for me today. He thanked me for the five silver coins I'd given him, and told me he would get started on my citizenship papers right away. We wished each other well and I walked off to the royal road alone, up the dirt road that led to the castle.

On my expedition earlier in the day, I hadn't gone that way, so I hadn't realized how difficult it was to traverse the royal road. It became steep at times, with loose gravelly rocks all about making it very difficult to trudge forward. I guessed that the road was meant to be that way to make it difficult for an invading army to reach the castle. It was a good safety feature in my assessment. I was sweating and breathing heavily at the exertion that came with the trek and I was less than halfway there.

Why couldn't they spare me a horse? I thought. It made me

angry. Not only was the climb difficult, but it took a longer time than necessary to reach my destination. That left me less time to bake my cookies, and I would have to make them while exhausted! Another thought immediately followed that one: King Sabrian was testing me. He was a man of great character. Certainly he wanted his subjects, particularly those in his service, to share in that character.

That didn't make me feel so bad, I supposed. Follow every good opportunity that presents itself- that was good advice, was it not? If that was the case, I could feel my character building with each aching step. After a long hour of walking I reached the mighty castle.

The castle was like a small town in itself. It had great fortified walls and a drawbridge, which was up. It was surrounded on all sides by a deep moat. By now it was probably seven in the evening, and I didn't know how to get into my kitchen! It could be anywhere within the building, of whose layout I knew nothing. "Hello there!" I called out, as I had at the south entrance this morning. "I'm Harold, the king's new baker! Please let me in!" There was no reply.

I picked up a small pebble and threw it at the door. It landed true. "Ahoy there! Please! Let me in! I'm to bake for the festival tonight! The Hunt Parade" I thought I was rather loud. And yet, there was still no reply. There was no movement of the drawbridge at all. Frustrated, I found a large rock on the ground and threw it at the drawbridge. It landed short, right in the moat. Plunk! After the rock hit the water I heard both the agitation of water and teeth snapping. The moat was filled with crocodiles, as moats are wont to do.

"The king awaits me! Please, open the bridge," I yelled. As if in reply, there was a sound from behind one of the many pillars. It sounded like a sigh of exhaustion, or perhaps frustration. This was followed by large mechanical gears grinding, and the drawbridge finally opening slowly.

Was it really a lazy soldier that hadn't wanted to let me in? Did he think I would just go away? Well, it is not in my nature to give up...even if today was the first day of my life. I decided I would forge my own nature, and decided to embrace the good parts of myself, of which there were a few. Tired, hungry, anxious, and now angry at lazy soldiers, I would do my job, and do it well. I felt almost noble.

As I entered the castle, I didn't stop to note anything that I saw. I tried to follow my nose directly to the kitchen. Following your nose is the wrong way to get anywhere unless you're a bear. There was hardly anyone there to ask directions, but eventually I found a maid, who told me where to go. When I entered, I was impressed by the sheer size of the kitchen. There were oil lamps set all about, so many that it almost seemed like daylight. To the rear of the kitchen was the pantry, from where I could take all the ingredients I required. It had everything.

And yet, there was something missing. Something big. Where was the full staff of fellow servants who were to help me with the baking? They were nowhere in sight. Was it possible they'd retired for the evening? If so, there were more lazy people in Mansfield than I'd ever imagined. Well, I couldn't be bothered with that. I had a job to do, help or no help.

Sugar- I needed sugar from the pantry. Sugar, flour, eggs, milk, honey, and various other extracts like cinnamon and tarot root. I took my ingredients and brought them all into the kitchen. Then I stopped for a moment, mapping out what I should make.

Yes, I got it, I thought. I could brew several cauldrons of tarot root tea with honey, and serve it with sugar cinnamon cookies. Then I could make dozens of apple and blueberry pies. That should be sufficient, and they were easy enough to make to be able to finish in time for the festival.

Now- if only I could find the cauldrons, pots, pans, knives, cups, spoons, and everything else that I needed before I went mad. Just before throwing my hands in the air in defeat, I heard a very innocent giggle coming from the entrance of the kitchen.

When I looked that way I saw a woman with searing green eyes laughing at me in good humor. She had hair the color of pure gold and wore a white dress. Her lips were thin and bright pink. All the other features were in my periphery- all I really, truly saw were her eyes. I was certain in that moment that I'd died and been greeted by an angel upon my passing.

Her emerald eyes struck me with a power that made me forget where I was or what I was doing. Indeed, I'd already forgotten myself through my amnesia, and peering into her soul through the windows of those eyes, brought me back to a beautiful oblivion.

Her words were the way warm pie tasted. Sweet and tart and lingering long after they were gone. "Hello there Harold. I'm Princess Hyacinth. When I heard we were to have a literate baker in our service, I simply had to come by to see for myself." She looked around at the state of affairs of the kitchen in which I was trying to navigate. She came to a very sensible conclusion. "This won't do. You have barely two hours to feed the kingdom, and it looks like our other servants took the rest of the night off. Let me help you."

I had so many questions about her- but of course they would have to wait. She was right, there was precious little time to make anything of worth to the people. Success on the day of my arrival would be good for me- a grand introduction to the rest of the population. Reputations are built and destroyed in mere moments, and I was thankful for the aid of the princess, who certainly knew her way around her own castle better than I.

I wasted precious little time once she entered. We worked rather well together. Up until then I'd only believed I could bake, but the proof is in the doing. Is the proof in the doing, or in the pudding? Did pudding exist yet?

I was learning new things about myself every moment. I

gave her very exact instructions. "Take six cups of sugar and mix it with this much flour. I'll beat a dozen eggs for this mixture."

"Yes, sir," she would reply, and then do what was asked without fail. She knew exactly what I wanted. Lady Hyacinth had no issues getting her dress dirty, either. It was very curious to me. Why would a princess know how to bake? Or even if she knew, why would she help a lowly trundle herb like me?

And then again, why would her half-sister join in military missions alongside the king? These were all questions to be asked after the baking and the serving is complete. The first thing is first- for the time being, there is nothing more important than the unmade cookies and pies before me. That which is unmade needs to be made after all.

Through a grand storm of activity, we rushed to finish our baking before the festival began. By 9:45 or so, we had completed our work. There were warm apple pies, sugar cinnamon cookies, cinnamon sugar cookies, lemon cookies, and several boiled pots of tarot root tea. It was nothing terribly fancy, but it was good. We tasted as we baked so we could assure its quality.

We had enough to fill a single large tray and a smaller tray. The princess took the small tray and I took the large one and we both walked down the loose gravel path. Two servants came with us, carrying the pies and tea kettles. They were the same two servants that took part in the Ogre Hunt and were about to be honored tonight.

Their names were Randolph and Brutus. Brutus was a sizable strongman with long hair and Roman features, particularly his nose. His hair was extremely curly and he wore no beard. Randolph, by comparison, was slimmer, and had lighter hair, a dark beard and very light eyes which were perhaps hazel-colored. They were recounting the events of the hunt to one another as if they'd caught ducks. The two of them walked together ahead of Princess Hyacinth and me.

"You're stronger than I would have guessed," she told me,

pointing at my heavy tray with her nose. It was a compliment, but I frowned as if insulted. She laughed and said, "I mean it in a good way."

My frown turned back to a smile. I felt as if I'd been smiling since I met her not two hours earlier. "Well, thank you, Princess. And thank you a thousand times for your help in making all this. There was no possible way that I could have done this without you."

She too, was stronger than she looked. The tray she carried was still heavy, although it was smaller. It was a silver tray, which is not a light metal.

"Coming to the aid of others is a pleasure for me, Harold. I'm happy to have helped, but you are too modest. This is your work, your vision. And if I may be so bold, it is quite a delicious vision indeed."

"You may be so bold. So, I beg your pardon for asking, but how is it that you know your way 'round a kitchen? Why learn how to bake or cook or make anything, when you can have servants to do it for you? I'd assume it's one of the finest perks of having royal blood."

The princess adjusted the tray, which was beginning to slip. "Because when others do things for you, they have some power over you, and you are always reliant upon them. I would rather not rely on powers greater than my own, if I can help it."

Mulling it over, I replied, "I can understand that, Princess. I apologize if I was rude in asking."

"Not at all. And please, call me Hyacinth. Hmm. Your question actually brings back warm memories to me. You see- the Queen was very self reliant and enjoyed doing so many things. I would cook and bake with her all the time. Queen Ophelia was a very good mother. She taught me well."

"I can see that, Prin--, Hyacinth. Sorry. I've never been on a first name basis with a princess before. That I can remember, at least."

She looked up towards Randolph and Brutus as if to make sure they were out of earshot. Then she readjusted her tray. "Well, I've always had some trouble with my title, Harold. Sabrian and Ophelia adopted me when I was a child. It's not exactly a secret but it's not exactly an oft-told story, but I was not their blood daughter.

"They found me, lost and abandoned in the woods, frightened and practically unable to speak. I was holding a hyacinth in my hands and babbling nonsense to myself. I didn't know who my parents were or how I came into the woods. So the king and queen took me in as their own and raised me as their daughter. I am a child of love, not blood. Two years or so after they found me, they were blessed with the birth of my sister, Syla. She is the real princess. She has all the high bearing of Ophelia."

Syla may be a princess, but she was not as regal as Hyacinth, I thought. "I'd imagine that love is lighter than air, and so it must weigh less than blood. Anything with weight can fall down if it is not held up. Love stays afloat, you see. In the course of our lives, nothing outside ourselves can cause it to fall, or fail. The love of your parents made you their daughter. And that, if you'll forgive me, makes you a 'real' princess, in my opinion."

Her light appeared to dim somewhat and her smile vanished. I could read from her expression that she was pained about something, and that it had something to do with Princess Syla and King Sabrian. Though we were having a heart-to-heart conversation, I was still a stranger. Come to think of it, she was still a stranger as well. We walked the rest of the way in silence. As we walked I noted how unstained her white dress remained through the entire course of baking, and by comparison how dirty I was.

Once we arrived to the festival, the merrymakers were all already drunk. We were greeted with cheers and ale. I'd put down my tray on a wooden table and Hyacinth put down hers. We could not help but laugh at the feeding frenzy that ensued. Everyone's hunger was ravenous- or perhaps this was the logical result of offering the king's food for free.

I had seen Brutus eat an entire apple pie all by himself. Before my attention was turned elsewhere, I could have sworn I saw him go back for another one. Gatekeeper Al was at the festival briefly. He clapped me on the shoulder and tipped his moth-eaten hat. "Delicious, Mister Baker. I must go home, early shift tomorrow, you know. That's why the two knights that were part of the hunting party aren't here- they'll be at the gate with me. Good night!"

There was much merriment and great conversation, all throughout the square. Joy was a happy contagion. Randolph and Brutus recounted the glorious tale of them killing two ogres and chasing away three others. Syla casually walked by and added, "Don't forget the troll I killed while you two were sleeping. Word will get around among their camp. For monsters, they do have quite a bit of fear. They won't be bothering us anytime soon."

She spotted Hyacinth at my side drinking a cup of tea and appeared pleasantly surprised. "Hello Hya. It's wonderful to see you here. I didn't think you came to these festivals any more."

Hyacinth nodded cordially at her sister. "Not only have I come, Sy, but I've brought treats. Our newest resident and I made them." She pointed at me. Syla seemed uninterested in me at all. Hyacinth changed the subject. "Where's Dad? Isn't he the man of the hour?"

Syla became more somber. It was a subtle change to her usual demeanor. "He never comes. He simply stays in his study and reads. He'll lead us in battle but not in celebration. It's left to me to be Mistress of Ceremonies." Syla was draped in royal blue and was wearing a thin silver crown. She bit into a cinnamon sugar cookie, then turned to me. "These are quite good. I want two for breakfast tomorrow." Kissing her sister on the cheek, she continued, "Now, if you'll excuse me, I must mingle with the nobles. Last chore of the festival. Good night." She curtsied to me and went on her way.

Once the fun was over, Hyacinth, Randolph, Brutus and I walked back uphill to the castle. Everyone was slightly inebriated. Some more than others, myself included. I hadn't recollected ever having that absent standing-still-but-spinning sensation, but I didn't like it. Not everything new is welcome. One should still keep their doors locked when Opportunity knocks. You must confirm that it's right and honest before you allow it to enter. Else it just may ransack everything.

The next day I awoke in my quarters. The servant's quarters were larger than the interior of a cottage. My bed was queen sized, and the bed sheets and bedcovers were all blue. There were wooden bureaus and nightstands to hold more items within them than I would ever possess.

I awoke at five in the morning and stayed in bed looking up at the perfectly manicured ceiling. The window to my right was open and I could see the sky was as dark as it was at midnight. There were wisps of clouds snaking through the stars. For some reason, it was enchanting. I could feel its thrall captivating me. And yet, I felt pulled to the kitchen. The baker's day begins early because breakfast is mere hours away. There is always a tremendous amount of preparation.

I washed up in my own basin with my own water, and headed to the kitchen. Other than lit torches lining the walls, there was no light at all in the entire castle. It was good that I wore my outer jacket, since stone walls retain terrible heat.

The kitchen seemed open and empty. Everything was washed and put away, probably by the night staff. There were so many servants in this place, I thought to myself. More than were needed. I'd thought that one copper piece per week was a pittance, but considering the large number of workers to be paid weekly, it is almost generous. Almost.

I found the flour, water, sugar and eggs in the back pantry. I located the cinnamon and the lemon and apples. I took tarot roots to boil for tea. I even took some almonds-I had a dream of making "almond cookies". Baking is an art, after all. However, baking seemed so lonely today.

Yet this was only the second time I could remember ever baking anything. This is the second day of my life that I actually remember at all. Two days in a row was not bad, I decided. Especially these last two; they were good days. Life is so short and no one knows how many days in a row there will be to ultimately remember.

I cracked open some eggs into a large bowl and began to beat them with an egg beater. As I went to pour the eggs into flour, I heard a loud whisper. "Harold! Good morning!" I nearly dropped my eggs. Turning, I saw Hyacinth, already washed and dressed for the day.

I whisper-yelled back, "Good morning, Hyacinth! Are you ready for another batch? I woke up with the crazy idea of adding almonds to the cookies and calling them 'almond cookies'. What do you think?"

She giggled. "I think that sounds like a wonderful idea. I bet they're just as good as your lemon cookies. My my, where do you come up with such extravagant ideas? You're quite the artist."

Her words lifted me up to the peak of the highest mountain. I was grateful for them. "I should be finished in a half hour or so- would you like to wait to have the first taste?"

She had a mischievous grin. I recognized it and fell deeply in love, as I had every moment in her presence. I didn't know that the speed of love was faster than time itself. She grabbed my forearms and said, "Why don't you put that flour down for the time being and join me in watching the sunrise? It's such a glorious experience and it passes so quickly. It's much better when shared with someone else."

I looked at the mess before me. So much left to be done. "When is sunrise?" I asked.

"In 45 minutes, an hour perhaps. But we have a bit of a trek.

The best view is from the northern lookout tower, which is at the top of the most beautiful hill."

I remembered that tower from my exploration the day earlier. That was more than an hour long trek! As if she read my mind, she said, "We'll need to go to the stables first and gather some horses." I bowed low in agreement.

After getting two white horses which were draped in blue and already saddled, I asked Hyacinth, "These are the knights' mounts, are they not?"

She nodded. "And why should only the knights be allowed to ride these magnificent creatures? The knights serve the realm, after all. And according to you, I am a true princess of the realm, so the knights serve me. As do their mounts, which they should have been guarding at this hour anyway."

Her reasoning was iron clad. I could not argue; I was busy looking into her green eyes. I looked away so as not to appear too enchanted by her. We rode up the hill past the few cottages all the way to the top. She patted her horse. "I call my mount Mayberry, after my childhood pet toad. You can tell Mayberry from this little spot on her cheek."

There were two knights at the lookout tower, at the ready. They saw us approach from afar. When we got close enough, one of them called down, "Good morning, melady. Sun's just about to go up. Ten minutes I reckon."

"Thank you, Sir Knight." We stationed our horses at the tower and walked the rest of the way. We walked north of the lookout tower, down the hill. We reclined on the hill as far east as we could possibly face, since the sun rises in the east and sets in the west. Odd how that happens on a flat Earth...

On that side of the hill were grimmle-berries growing from berry bushes and moonlock growing in between those bushes. Moonlock and grimmle-berries were both rare and NEVER grew together, I was sure. But I did not know why.

I went to touch a leaf of the moonlock; it was almost silver in color. It was spiky and leafy, like leaves of holly. Yet it felt softer than it looked. Hyacinth, watching me caress the herb, stopped me from making a big mistake. "You can touch the moonlock as long as you don't bring it back with you to make tea. Not many outsiders know this, but moonlock is a very potent plant. It puts you into a deep sleep for one hundred years. It's why there are no cottages on this side of the hill- no one is foolish enough to come here."

"Except us," I pointed out. There was a sweet scent in the air, but I couldn't tell if it came from the grimmle-berry bushes or the moonlock. They were so intertwined. Though I hadn't seen much in my couple of days of continuous memory, I was certain of the rarity of the two plants living together. What a shame that moonlock was so toxic. It would have probably made a fine tea.

"Does no one eat these grimmle-berries then?"

Hyacinth looked sideways at me. "Grimmle-? We haven't even named those other plants. We've just assumed they were too dangerous to eat by association. Now, take a look at the beautiful horizon out there. Doesn't it feel like you can almost see everything there is? Like everything in the world is in front of you, and the sun is about to illuminate it. Do you see the line of orange breaking through there? As far as the eye can see. The light beginning to reflect off the mountains in the distance. And the stars above, about to vanish in a moment. It's as if every morning, the night dies. And every dusk, the day dies."

"Interesting that you see it as a death rather than a rebirth."

"I think it can only be reborn if it dies first. It's a beautiful thought, to me." She looked at me and at that moment, the sun began shining up the hill, banishing the night completely. Her eyes shone like gems in the light. Like perfect emeralds, their fire danced with the rising tide of day.

And just at that moment, I could not help myself; I was over-whelmed with a powerful smile in my heart. I kissed her. I kissed the princess! The more exciting aspect of that fact is that she kissed me back. It was a passionate kiss, and it felt good in the romantic dew of morning. It was my first and best kiss.

I pulled away. "Princess, I'm sorry, I lost control of my senses."

She took out a fan and waved it jocularly. "As did I, Harold. But like I said, call me Hyacinth." She put her delicate hand in mine and we walked through the many hidden parts of the northern hill. There was an apple orchard that belonged to the king, and a secondary garden. As we walked, we talked about this or that. It was as if the morning warmed us into waking, like we were as alive and aflame as the sun itself.

"So, Hyacinth. Permit me to ask- why is it you don't usually go to festivals?"

"Oh, that. That question, which I saw forming in your mind last night, you decide to ask now that you are emboldened by my kiss? Well, I can tell you- I do go to the festivals. The harvest festival, the spring festival, the winter festival. What I usually do not attend, are the festivals in honor of the war parties' 'hunts'. For one thing they are dangerous and unnecessary, and my father and sister always go, unconcerned that they might not come back if things go wrong. It's selfish. They wouldn't just be leaving me behind in mourning, but the entire kingdom."

We continued walking and holding hands, even as we clambered over streams and rocks and slippery stones. We were in a very small forest at the bottom of the hill, near the boundary wall. "I can only imagine it is their way to honor your mother's memory, by trying to protect the very realm she saved with her life. Whether it is misguided or not, the intentions of your father and sister come from there. You said, 'for one thing.' What is the other reason you are upset about it?"

She looked exasperated. "Because it's barbaric! They go out and seek slaughter for its own sake. Defending the realm is one thing, and if it came to it, I would grab a sword and shield and fight alongside them. But to hunt living and thinking creatures out of an abnormally heightened sense of fear is irrational.

Without discovering if they are friend or foe, the war parties chase and often kill our 'enemies'. It is not right, and I cannot bring myself to celebrate it. I came last night as a rare sign of alignment to that cause. I must show my allegiance to the realm and the general defense of its people. Heaven forbid, If Sabrian and Syla should ever die in battle, I am to be their queen after all."

I pushed away a tree branch from both of us so we could pass. We were on our way back up the hill. I pointed out to her, "The king, too, stays away from the festivals. Perhaps he is tortured by his decision to do what he feels is the right thing. Perhaps he is a reluctant hero in all this. Maybe he knows on some level that it's wrong."

She shook her head, but then nodded. "He is a good man. My sister is also good. And maybe in this, they are right. But it does not feel right to me. My father doesn't stay away from celebration because of any political reason. I learned from Syla that he's been holed up in the royal archives every night, reading and studying the magic manuscripts. Although magic has been forbidden in all of Mansfield, he wants to be prepared in case of an attack from magic sources. If he is the only practitioner of magic within these borders, then he feels safer that its knowledge is in good hands."

It was the height of hypocrisy for sure, but I was no one to judge a king. The weight of that crown is a heaviness only the wearer knows. Only the wearer can bear it. They are burdened with the responsibility, and charged to do the right thing in all circumstances, no matter how murky or muddled.

"What about you?" Hyacinth asked from within a looming silence.

"What about me?" I mirrored back.

"In a day I've told you more than my friends know about me, and yet you tell me nothing of yourself. Where do you hail from? How did you learn to bake? What is your favorite food?"

I paused. When she asked me that I had a frightening thought. Since I didn't remember more than two days ago, and am already a grown man, what is it that I've left behind? Could I have a family, replete with wife and children, waiting for me somewhere? And yet, I did not feel pulled in any other direction. I felt strongly as if I belonged here in Mansfield, especially with the princess.

"My favorite food is grimmle-berry pie. I learned to bake when I was younger. My past...is full of emptiness, if I'm to be honest. Awaken, go to work, go to sleep. Wake up, work, sleep. It was so routine that my life before arriving here might as well have not happened." I cleared some strands of hair from her face. Then I kissed her again.

"The more I think about it, the more that now matters, more than any other time." I caressed her cheek. I was happy and overwhelmed. The greatest bards and minstrels could not describe the feeling of undeserved luck and appreciation I had, that she appeared as enchanted by me as I was by her.

We decided to court and take things slowly. We would tell no one of our newly budding romance, at least not until it grew into something more lasting. The two of us wanted to make sure this mutual interest could become love, and both daringly hoped it did.

CHAPTER 3

It did. Though my memory hadn't yet returned, the next couple of months were magical without need of any potions, spells or incantations. I settled into my role both as servant baker of the royal house and as suitor to Princess Hyacinth. My status as her loving companion was still a secret, but something of an open one.

It was nearly mid-November. Gatekeeper Al secured my citizenship to Mansfield, as promised. In a ceremony including several other servants and prominent members of our society, I swore an oath before the king to renounce all previous loyalties. With my hand firmly on my heart I promised to protect the realm of Mansfield, and its king, and its royal house, and all its people. It was a proud day for me, one I intended to cherish and remember forever.

I was invited by Al to say a few words before the crowd opened the celebratory ale. I'm unsure how the words came out or sounded, since I was faced with yet another new emotion- fear of public speaking. Yet I do recall the meaning behind them. I told the listeners that my first day in the kingdom, two paltry months ago, my king requested I walk up the difficult path to the castle that would be my home, and my workplace.

I told the listeners that my king was truly wise in teaching me the most invaluable lesson of life: it is in walking the difficult path, that we best arrive to where we're going. The journey, the destination, are both meaningless if I do not appreciate them.

I can only appreciate my blessings by reflecting on my effort in achieving what the world allows, but does not promise. Then I bent on my knee with my fist on my heart, toward the king and his daughters. "I am proud to be a citizen."

Next week was the harvest feast, which meant that this entire week was the harvest. Servants of the castle could choose whether to join the harvest or the new Dragon Hunt. Dragons were sighted to the far east of the East Woods, and were considered more dangerous than ogres because of their greater size and ability to fly. Legend told of dragons having other mystical powers, but they were so rare that it was unknown what these specific creatures could do.

If ill-intentioned, dragons could not only barrel directly into Mansfield, but also attack it from above. At once and in great haste, King Sabrian assembled the people into the great square to ask for volunteers. He was a just and a fair ruler, and truly listened to the desires of his people. And yet he knew any decision needing to be made would be made by him alone.

An older man had asked him, "But the dragons are yet so far away- how do we know they will come to harm us?"

The King's reply was simple. "It is better to fight enemies as far from your walls as possible, because if you fight them within your walls, you're not fighting- you're defending, and that is already a position of weakness. A position, I might remind, we were in once before and one I swore never to be in again."

I chose to partake in the harvest, picking fruits and reaping crops. Hyacinth was against my volunteering to join any hunts. When I made my decision, the king looked at me with such fire that I thought I would char and blacken.

My soul was singed, however. At that moment I knew that Sabrian was aware of my relationship with his daughter, and that he wanted me to join him in glorious battle for her sake. I saw disappointment and shame in his eyes, but then he closed them, and passed by me.

Randolph and Brutus elected to fight, as they always did when the challenge came. It appeared that the future for both of them was to become soldiers, guards, or knights. Or perhaps they were simply good at fighting dragons and ogres. It was not a bad occupation for a citizen of Mansfield, it seemed.

We had all three become friends, but I was much closer to Randolph. There was something familiar and comforting about him. He was a good man with a strong character, which I admired very much. Brutus seemed good too, but he seemed to be more of a child of chaos.

When they had learned of my mutual affection for the princess, they had mixed reactions. Randolph, as was his nature, was genuinely happy for me. He told me he'd buy me a pitcher of ale to celebrate our union and our future. Brutus said he was happy with his words, but had not come to the pub to celebrate with us. Since then, he's spoken little to me.

The night before the hunt was another festival, the Dragon Hunt Send-off. In that celebration, townspeople who did not volunteer would wish the hunting party well. Some would give gifts, like food, water, weapons, or hunting supplies. I gave food-bread that I made for the entire group of about forty people. Ironsmiths and blacksmiths donated weapons and armor. There were many spears and poison-tipped arrows among them.

We all offered up our good intentions and our loyalty. The king reviewed with all of us our standing orders in time of such great peril. If the need were to become dire, the women and children would be shepherded into the castle dungeons, where they would be safest. All the able-bodied men in the realm, myself included, would be required to don armor and weapons from the king's armory and fight alongside our army, which was commanded by the Order of Seven Knights. These were the highest ranking knights in the land, in command of fifty knights below them. The knights in turn coordinated all other soldiers and guards.

It was a sobering and majestic spectacle to bear witness to such camaraderie and unity among people.

Before the night ended, we all held hands in a circle around a great fire, and asked the spirits that our brave warriors might be protected in their quest. We sang:

Let those who protect the realm rejoice,
The gathering winds, their thunderous voice
And the enemies of the realm to dwell
In the darkest pit of the blackest hell.
Facing danger Mansfield shan't fear it
Carrying with them the might of their spirit.
May they bring calamity to their foe,
With all the realm's power wrapped in each blow.
And rising beyond the battle we see
A new dawn, the sight of victory.

The day of the hunt began early. All volunteers went out through the one main door to the south. There were extra sentries at the north and south lookout towers and also a battalion of soldiers stationed at the East and West. Should the hunting party need assistance, or fail in their quest, the extra soldiers would launch a full strike against the dragons at once. These soldiers were our front-line defense. If they were dispatched, it meant we should move women and children to safety and grab a sword ourselves.

Each lookout tower had a large fire pit full of kindling, hay, and dry, slow-burning wood. In case of any important event, the pit is lit as a beacon. Then the guards would sprinkle dust over the fire which burns a particular color. If the fire burns red, that means danger. It's a sign for the warriors to assemble and mobilize. Blue fire, however, means victory. It's a sign of triumph over the enemy. Whenever the beacon is lit with any color, a horn also sounds. All the worried villagers paid attention to the beacon day and night for updates.

Every hour on the hour a cry would ring out, "All is well!" I could hear it from the fields while picking fruits. I was assigned to the royal vineyards, collecting and crushing grapes. I worked the vineyards during the day, and in the kitchen morning and night for breakfast and dessert.

Hyacinth and I worried for the safe return of her father and sister. I'd also worried about my friends and fellow servants. Dragons were very dangerous. Every morning of the harvest week, we would both watch the sunrise from near the north lookout tower. The watchers had eagle eyes and could see much farther than we, so we'd always ask them what was going on with the hunt. Most of the time they told us that the hunting party was simply waiting, camped out in front of a fire. The watchers saw no sign of the dragons since the very first sighting that launched the expedition.

Then on the last day of the harvest, in the middle of the day, the great horn sounded, first from the southern tower and then from the north. I ran from the vineyard, and saw that the beacon fire was blue. It was a glorious feeling of pride to see the blue beacon shine. For five minutes I simply watched it and cried.

I ran to the castle, and with my beloved we waited for the victorious warriors that somehow overwhelmed their dragon foes. They came through the doors with great animation, carrying both Randolph and Brutus on their shoulders. They must have been especially valiant in battle.

Though I did not fully agree with the preemptive strike, I was relieved at the outcome. As well as surprised by it. Dragons are overwhelming creatures. Forty armed soldiers seemed almost a flimsy defense, and yet they prevailed. Needless to say, we had a celebration in the main square.

Although she rarely attended these kinds of events, Hyacinth made sure to celebrate the safe return of her family, and the other fighters. The warriors that were on this mission were cobblers, millers, candlestick makers- in short, they were laborers that fought for the safety of their kingdom. Hyacinth was always quick to show appreciation for those that give more than their due. The quality of the citizenry was perhaps the biggest reason I was happy to have found Mansfield and overjoyed to be a small part of it. I was happy to be a contributor.

I'd baked cakes and all kinds of assorted confections. I was truly branching out and growing into a masterful artist, if I may say so myself. Hyacinth also said so, as did the many merrymakers in the square. Gatekeeper Al did not, because he was suspiciously absent from the affair. I hoped he was well.

Throughout the commotion, I had such a strange and lingering thought. Would it not have been funny to add spicy pepper to the cookies and cakes, and watch everyone's reaction as they spit out the abomination? Or to have used ants, or bees, instead of raisins? The look of surprise on everyone's faces would have been marvellous. Quite satisfying. And as that thought rose up in my mind, another thought rose along with it, like yeast leavens bread- "No, it becomes ye not."

The king attended this event, since it was of a greater magnitude than a pedestrian ogre hunt. It was also the harvest festival by coincidence- a time to eat, drink, be merry, and eat and drink some more. He sounded the great horn, to bring us all to attention. We stopped what we were doing and listened. Hyacinth was by my side, handing out sugary treats to children. She too, stopped to listen.

"My fellow countrymen and women, and all you little children. Today is a proud day for all of us. Today is a day we can all look back on with feelings of peace, security, unity, and feeling that our little kingdom on a hill, is thriving. Our harvest this year was our biggest in a decade. We have wine and grain for years to come. No one among us will go hungry this winter. These are good times, made better by the people you see before you, who chose to represent you in a glorious fight against evil.

"For some time now, we have known we are often the targets of powerful enemies. And that the best course for us to take is to meet them head-on. We have prevailed time and again, because we do not fight alone- every one of you here is with us on the battlefield. We feel your presence, and it goads us into action. Each one of these volunteers deserves to be honored tonight and evermore, simply for choosing to join the dragon hunt. For choosing to be heroes." King Sabrian looked at me, then at Hyacinth, and then paused. "You all who carried us are also heroes, so applaud yourselves as I applaud you."

Applause rose to a raucous rancor down to a cricket's single chirp. He looked around and continued.

"Yet, there are two who stood above the rest. Two whose bravery brought defeat upon the dragons." His voice changed as he recounted the tale. It became more of a narrative than a speech. "It was our seventh day camped out where the creatures were first sighted. We hadn't seen them in all those seven days but we knew they were there. We remained patient in our ranks, biding our time. We hunted, fished, and foraged as the enemy took its time showing itself.

"We knew the dragons were sighted just outside of The Sleepy Cave in the East, the largest cave we know of in Europe. After waiting such a long time, we thought that they might be sleeping, as dragons sleep for fortnights on end. We decided to scout, and go into their cave to see what was going on. Randolph and Brutus volunteered to be advance scouts- to enter the cave and find where the beasts were sleeping. Our plan was to map out where they slept and then swoop in like the angel of death to slay the lot of them.

"And when these scouts entered, my friends, but of course you must know by now- the beasts were not asleep. Far from it. There were three of them. And seeing our scouts, they were enraged to have their sovereignty disturbed. We saw Brutus and Randolph run out of the cave, billows of fire and smoke chasing after them. The biggest brute, the leader among them, caught up with them in one wide leap. He blew fire that somehow wrapped around Brutus in a great circle, trapping them together surrounded by a wall of flame.

"The rest of us couldn't see the fight since the wall was high up to the skies. We heard a great clamor from within as Brutus clashed with the demonspawn. It appeared the demon was winning when to our amazement, we all saw Randolph jump into the flames to help his comrade. And when the dust settled and the fire went out, our two heroes remained standing, and the great dragon had been slain. Its robust exterior belied its soft underbelly.

"Witnessing their fallen leader at our feet, the two others flew off into the distance with great fear and trembling. And then, a most surprising thing happened. The dead dragon vanished in a great puff of black smoke, as if it had been blown off from the cauldron of Hell by the Devil himself."

The King was quite the wordsmith. He motioned to all the fighters with a wave of his hand.

"And so, without further delay, it is my honor as well as should be yours, to welcome all your brave citizens back into your lives, but to especially celebrate the newest knights of the realm, Randolph and Brutus! They will be honored in a separate ceremony and be made official in one week's time."

Everyone clapped enthusiastically at the king's story, and at the men of the hour. But just as the commotion began to die down, there was more. The king raised both his hands in the air to hush the crowd in order to express an even greater bit of news.

"Because I have never in my entire life seen such bravery, and because of the immense loyalty of these men, who just a week ago were humble servants- I have added them both to the Order of Seven Knights. It shall henceforth be known as the Order of Nine Knights, who answer only to my command, and who control our venerable defense apparatus."

There was a hush among the crowd, since this manner of promotion was without precedent. These were servants, outsiders until a mere five months ago.

"I urge you all to give these fine gentlemen your own personal congratulations and gratitude whenever you see them. Now, get back to your fun! Eat, drink, make merry. It's harvest time!"

The King shook hands with each of the volunteers, and then quickly mingled with the impatient nobility. After some apparent small talk, he left them as well and went back to the castle. We continued feeding guests at the party until well into the night. Before we were quite out of all our food, Gatekeeper Al came walking by, with a plump older woman at his side. She had blond curly hair, and blue eyes the color of twilight.

He tipped his ratty hat. "Mister Baker, good harvest to thee. This is my wife, Haglinda. I told her a bit about ye. Told her ye've got the best baked goods in all Europe, Near East, Far East, and New World, for that matter. If there is one out there, that is. What would I know of such things?"

Attempting to be a perfect gentleman, I took Haglinda's hand and kissed it, bowing ever so slightly in respect. She curtsied like a young woman would, very graciously. "How d'ye do good sire? I don't much liss'n to me husband but I gotta say fer meself, yer food is the best in the land. I would surely love to git a recipe someday but alas, I can't read. Me husband can though, did ye know that?"

I nodded humbly at her. Al blushed. "That I did, my lady. He is both a very intelligent and a very good man."

Haglinda looked at her husband, and then at me. "Bah. Good, bad. Them's just words. They change dependin' on who's lookin' and who's saying 'em. And when they're lookin' and talkin'. All of us is good and bad some time er other."

81

Her poor grammar belied her wisdom. She was right. Behind all people there is another face. It is like a living painting, with the colors changing day to day, even moment to moment. Good and evil, creation and destruction, were all possible in every soul. Not only possible, but existing side by side.

"And who's yer lovely wife over there, helpin' ye out with the food? Why is that the Princess? Oh goodness, me lady, it is ye!" Rather than a polite curtsy this time, she genuflected. To me she then also bowed. "And that means ye will be our next Prince. Me lord." Gatekeeper Al, prodded by his wife, also bowed to us both, but it was more of a nod, a type of how-ye-do. He sees us every day, after all.

Hyacinth and I looked at each other, the corners of our mouths rising ever so slightly. We bowed back to the couple, and didn't argue with Haglinda's assessment. I hadn't even considered what would become of us eventually, but it was true. If I married the Princess, I'd become a Prince. How great, and alarming, and beautiful, and frightening.

Eventually we were down to our last piece of the last apple pie. Brutus had eaten the lion's share of that. It was not only the last piece of pie, but also the last morsel of food we'd made. Usually throughout the festivals, we'd always have several things left over which would easily be wrapped up for the king's breakfast. But this time we ran completely out. Save that one slice.

The drunk redhead I'd met during my first day here walked up to me. I hadn't seen him much about town and I was plenty sure he didn't remember me. Drunk as is customary for him, the man stumbled over to me and asked for the piece. He less asked than flubbered. "Gladly," I replied, with an intentional tone of over-eager courtesy. My intention was to pick it up and drop it into the mud at his feet, and then feign sorrow at my clumsy mistake.

But at that moment, Haglinda picked up the piece and handed it over to the man with an effervescent smile. "Thought

I'd help and be good fer somethin' at least," she said to me with her words. What she said with her eyes, however, seemed to be, "don't do that- it becomes ye not."

Although the night ended late, we both arose before dawn. We cleaned up and went out to the north hill for the best view of the coming morning. We walked in happy silence until we reached the foot of the hill. "So, did that woman frighten you off with her prediction of marriage and children and prince-ship?"

I squinted my eyes at her. "She didn't mention children!" I teased. But she did mention becoming a prince. All at once I lost my breath, and felt as if the dying night sky were crushing my chest. I became upset at the thought. It's not the marriage part-- I would have married Hyacinth yesterday if it were possible. Nor is it the children part-- I find that I like children, and the thought of having them with her makes it even more wonderful.

It's the becoming a prince part that spun me in circles. And when Sabrian dies, perhaps even king. Such is to also be the fate of my own child. I could not bear the thought! All the responsibility and power would be too much, commanding others and being charged with their care. It was a duty and a burden I wished on others with stronger shoulders and bigger backs.

Randolph and Brutus were given the task of manning the post of the Northern lookout tower. Technically, the King proclaimed them knights and so, knights they were. And yet, they wore the uniforms of simple guards- a helmet, light chain mail, gauntlets and leather boots, with the golden-hawked crest of the great seal on their chests. Perhaps they were on probation until their inauguration.

"Ahoy there you two! You must promise us you'll outdo yourselves for the reception after the knighting ceremony," Randolph called down to us. Brutus simply smirked and picked his teeth with a carving knife.

"Make a lot of that apple pie," Brutus said eventually, looking out and scanning the horizon. They seemed to both be comfortable in their posts, as naturally as squirrels take to the trees.

Either one of them could be king, I thought.

The next few months were pleasant and uneventful, in my opinion. I spent the mornings and days with my beloved, and in the course of my labor which was beginning to make me weary. I began to dream of a life beyond baking, a greater calling. Perhaps it was time to consider a change of some kind. Pleasant and uneventful could rapidly turn into...boring. That is, until something eventful and frightening happens, which it inevitably does. How we long for boring then.

Not much news ever comes through Mansfield, but the recent chatter about town has been alarming. There seem to be a growing number of strange "attacks" on people which made no sense. Contrary to a popular tale involving helpful elves, a cobbler awoke to find all of the shoes he'd prepared for customers singed to a leathery crisp. Some farmers reported their cows having been milked overnight, right onto the grass. The animals hadn't any at all left in them the next day. This happened for nearly a week.

And the strangest thing to happen was that an old widow had received three children on her doorstep in the middle of the night one frigid Friday. It was good that she'd heard the door knocking because if she hadn't, the poor things would have frozen. The biggest problem with receiving the children was that there was no milk with which to feed them! The farm nearest to her was milked dry. Either way, she could not pay the premium for a waning supply from distant farms.

The woman brought all three of them to the royal castle to be fed by the king's ample store. There is a great surplus kept there for emergencies. Sometime later, three women also went to the castle to file a claim that their children had been kidnapped.

The children were returned to their rightful mothers. People were frightened about a prowler or prowlers with a mischievous

84

sense of humor roaming around in their great kingdom. There was almost no criminality in Mansfield, since everyone seemed dedicated to serving the kingdom in their own way. The bakers bake, the smiths smith, the millers mill, and the innkeepers keep inns. Danger always came from the outside, or so we all thought.

The royal guard doubled their nightly patrols to prevent anything like this happening again. Brutus and Randolph oversaw their own battalions, which they activated to search Mansfield both high and low. There were teams of knights at the north, east, west and south, and in the center were extensions of the royal guard. The first night that the extra security was deployed, nothing happened.

As a matter of fact, nothing happened for almost an entire month of elevated alert. As time passed, things returned to business as usual. The extra security was gradually reduced and then removed altogether.

The night that the extra patrol was pulled, more such mischievous things happened. However, they seemed to be more malicious now than the first time. Malice and mischief are often easy to confuse. The line between them is not readily apparent, and often quite blurred. The chief manifestation of mischief is disruption. It is meant to cause detours, to make others go off course. Malice is similar, but the main difference is that the disruption causes greater harm. Irreversible harm. Its disruption is more potent, and is done for more devious reasons. Malice is cruel while mischief is not.

The next day, all the cows from all the farms within our borders had been milked. Even the great stores of milk intended to be kept for winter were drained from the farms as well. The grass was soaked white.

The cobbler who a month earlier awoke to his shoes having been burnt, awoke this time to shoes glued over his hands and feet. Shoe glue was very strong and there was no antidote to it. He'd told his wife that he dreamed he was being tortured by a malevolent imp, who had stuck shoes on him, and woke up to find it was true.

Throughout the land, many people were reporting that they too, had terrible dreams of an imp persecuting them, and in the morning, they found their dream to be reality. Some women dreamed their children were taken from them and they were gone the next day. This time there was no old woman to whom the children went, so they were actually missing, no one knowing where.

King Sabrian tripled the guard this time. There was almost the entire army deployed within the kingdom's walls. Even the full Order of Nine was deployed. Brutus was in the West Woods and Randolph was in the East Woods on a 24 hour patrol. Brutus asked the king, "Who will guard the royal archives? I volunteer myself and my men should you need, my lord."

The king replied, "I guard the archives myself. And when I am not there, a powerful enchantment protects it. The archives are safe. The enchantment states that only the king and those given explicit access to it by the king are allowed to traverse its boundary. You are best employed in the woods, since imps are forest creatures. Report back daily."

"As you wish my lord. Who would have thought we'd have imps among us?" Brutus then lead about thirty men westward. The king walked away and went upstairs into his quarters. They had been speaking in one of the many great halls of the castle, near to the kitchen. I'd heard every word.

As did Hyacinth, who has been helping me in the kitchen ever since our first kiss. "These are troubling times," I told her. "It's unsettling to fear such things in the dark. Your father is very brave." I continued churning butter as I spoke to her. I had eggs at the ready on the countertop, waiting to be beaten.

Hyacinth nodded. "It might not even be imps! So some people had some strange dreams- so what? It doesn't always have to be magical. There are bad people out there as well. Human beings are dreadfully flawed; we are not perfect. I fear that someday, he will find great danger from within from our very own kind. What will he do then?" I wiped a tear from her perfect cheek.

She continued. "He is very brave. And stubborn. He is quick to fight, even when he is outmatched. We've never seen imps in our land and don't know what they are capable of. But I know he would pursue a war with them if he believed us to be in any kind of danger. He never attempts diplomacy first."

I wanted to be tactless but firm and understanding. "Diplomacy killed your mother," I noted. "At least from his point of view. At that time of the great attack, he had everything to lose, as king and as father and husband. And now, he still has everything to lose. Nothing's changed in that sense. Except for his experience. He won't make the same mistake twice. Again—from his perspective, how can he be doing wrong by protecting his own?"

She was tearing up. The familiar memories of her mother, perhaps. Or maybe what I'd said struck a chord with her. "That's just it. He does not know the line. He does not know when to fight and when to negotiate. Sometimes fighting is worse. No matter that we won the battle against the dragons. It could have turned out differently, it could have easily not been so. The entire hunting party could have all died! Why provoke a dragon? And in this case now, why provoke creatures we know nothing about, whether in ability, or in how they are likely to react to us?"

I waved my hand. "Imps are harmless," I reassured her, as if I knew that was true. Well, something in my heart did tell me that it was true. Most of the time, at least. Except when they do things like they apparently did. "They were probably just fooling around and didn't know when to stop."

She put down the sugar that she was mixing into flour. "They kidnapped children and destroyed part of our food supply. It sounds more malicious than simply fooling around. My fear is both, what we're facing, and how my father will react to it. He always says you have to meet your obstacles as far from home as you can. But they are here already! Which means our fair land is to be our battleground."

I stopped beating my eggs and went over and kissed her. She worries because she cares immensely. These are her people and she feels responsible for them. She wants what is best for them but cannot simply will it to happen. It is hard to know what to do and do it. The actions that are needed to make change- those are difficult to divine, and even more difficult to enact.

I had to make her sorrow go away. I could not bear the weight of her heavy heart. "Don't worry, my love. It won't come to that. I promise you that if there's anything at all I can possibly do to fix this, I will make it go away." She flitted her eyes as she gently pulled from my embrace. Looking behind me, her eyes widened as if startled. She withdrew from me completely.

"Oh, father! I didn't know you were here. Would you like some breakfast?"

Sabrian sat himself slowly at the table. He pulled a chair. "Yes I would, Hyacinth. But I will not be served by you. Go back to your chambers. I wish to speak to Mister Baker. Alone. All of you, head back to your quarters at once." He motioned to the other servants to leave. I have to admit, I often forgot the others were there, since for the most part, they were completely unhelpful. They scattered in a hurry, not from fear, but I suspect from elation at getting the time off.

Hyacinth also left, after bowing to her father and then to me. I pretended the king was not irate. "Shall I make you some scrambled eggs with lean bacon, your highness?"

He seemed to soften immediately. "Yes, you know scrambled eggs are my favorite breakfast. And adding bacon makes the eggs somewhat divine." He scratched his head. It became apparent that he didn't quite know how to approach me. "Harold, you know that I am a king of the people. I don't lord anything over them. I appreciate the service of others and have a strong belief in rewarding those that work hardest and show the most loyalty. That having been said, I am also a father." He stood up and began to pace slowly, as if finding the words floating in the air and plucking them like daisies.

"I know that you and Hyacinth are in love. As a father, it warms my heart to see my daughter happy. But I need to know she is with the right kind of man."

I was puzzled and offended. Both were things I'd have to keep to myself. "Have I been less than good to her, my lord?"

He shook his head and his crown displaced itself briefly. "No, you are a good man, Harold. I would never say otherwise. You care a great deal about Hyacinth, and it shows in how you treat her. But she is a princess." He looked over to the spot Hyacinth just was, helping me to knead dough. "Not a baker's aid. And when I die, she is the eldest daughter, adopted or not. She will be the queen. She and her husband must protect the realm with the passion and fervor with which I and my youngest daughter Syla, do."

I began to cook the eggs as humbly as possible. Sabrian must have heard us from the hallway speaking about the imps. The walls echo and are rife with secrets. I didn't know what to say, precisely. I'd been in Mansfield for five months, and had already seen ogre hunts, dragon hunts, and soon, I'd see imp hunts. Only the ogres had actually provoked the kingdom, and their attack was repelled. And yet, the ogres killed in the subsequent hunt may have been from a completely different tribe. An overprotective king does not see the difference from one to the other. Is this a common human flaw, like color blindness?

He sighed with breath he seemed to have held for a thousand years. "It might appear from the outside that I'm a war monger, someone who loves to go into glorious battle. That I enjoy the thrill of it. The truth is that it is wearying, and I am always reluctant to put myself, my daughter, my men, in danger when I go. But I go anyway, because I have seen firsthand how others might take your goodness, and twist it into something terrible. How quickly worlds can crumble. It may mean having a quick trigger sometimes, but a quick trigger saves lives. Ask any archer anywhere.

"We do what we must to stay safe. It is always a fight for survival, especially being situated where we are. We are at the crossroads of many realms, which means we are lucky not to be constantly bombarded all the time. The magical creatures around us hear legends of our archives and the knowledge contained within. They want to steal them, in order to gain the upper hand over their other enemies. It is magical espionage and we are in the middle of their doings. We cannot live in peace because they will not let us. Then in other instances it's a matter of hunger, like ogres or heaven forbid, werewolves. We have food and they want food." He plunked down into his chair, tilted his head in my direction and pointed a strong finger at me.

"Harold, we are always in danger. And the fact that most days you can breathe easy and go for morning walks without a care, shows just how good I am at protecting you. Your freedom to go about your daily routine is hard-fought."

I finished frying the eggs in lard and scrambling them. I put them on a plate with similarly fried bacon, added two muffins, then handed it to the king. "What is it that you wish me to do, Lord Sabrian? I would do anything for Hyacinth's hand. Whatever I must do to obtain your blessing, I will."

Sabrian pointed behind me. "Some tea please, Harold."

"Tarot root, chamomile, or black tea?"

"Tarot root, with a hint of cinnamon and a lemon wedge. I must say, that combination is excellent. You truly are an inspired artist." He shoveled a spoon's scoop of scrambled eggs into his mouth and then took a bite of the muffin. "But I need you to be more. For her. And someday for this kingdom. I need you to be a warrior for peace. You are strong, much stronger than you look. If this problem with the imps turns into a war or a hunt or if it requires any kind of military action, I want you to volunteer. That is all. It shows loyalty, and strength of conviction. And for the people, if you are to be their king someday, they must see you fight for them."

I bowed low, as low as I could, and felt my knee hit the floor. My right arm was draped across my chest and my head was down. I swore fealty and pledged my commitment to the cause of protection. King Sabrian appeared pleased. "It would be my wish to knight you someday. Knights show extraordinary devotion, and that kind of person is exactly who I want my daughter to be with." He looked into my dark eyes with his soft, blue ones. He meant it. His eyes were a lighter hue than I'd previously thought.

The next time I had occasion to see Hyacinth was the next morning when we stood witness to the rise of the sun. I marvelled that we'd seen so many sunrises together- in the rain, in perfect weather, through a great fog, in the finest dew, while happy and also while sad. We hardly ever speak until we arrive at the hill since our minds are still wrapped in cobwebs of sleep.

Sometimes we walk, hand in hand. That is, when we leave early enough. Most of the times we steal unguarded horses from the royal stable, which we return before their absence is questioned.

She was patient as always this morning. The sun came up fully, first a sliver, then a wedge, then a sphere, before she asked me what the king wanted with me. I told her that the king let me know he was aware of our love and of my intentions to marry. And that he wanted to make sure I would be good to her. I said that if I remained good to her, I'd have his blessing.

She sighed in a lovely way. "He has always been tough on my suitors. You're the first one that isn't a knight or a guard, or a noble's son."

"You've had others?" I asked with undue incredulity.

She motioned to her body and her face. "Of course! You forget, I own a mirror, unlike most people in this day and age. I know what I look like. Daily. Sometimes hourly."

"What was wrong with the other suitors, if you don't mind my asking?" I pretended to busy myself with the laces of my boots. Jealousy has an ugly face, and unfortunately it was the second face that I was currently wearing.

She ate up my jealousy as if it were one of my famous raspberry tarts. "The other suitors had more...ambitious hearts. They all wanted to become king. When trying to woo me, they did not see me, they saw the crown. You are different. You love me, truly and without any other motives. You actually seem to be quite shy of the crown. What's wrong with the others, was that they were not enough like you. Devoted. Adoring. And kind. With a little bit of a mischievous quality boiling just below the surface. I can see it in your eyes when you smile." She looked my face up and down. "It's very boyish and charming." She fixed my hair, as I had fixed hers, right before our first kiss. But our next kiss was not to be...at least not just yet.

The great horn sounded from the northern lookout tower. It was followed by a horn sounding far away from the southern tower. A third horn also then sounded from the castle. When we looked at the beacon, it was already lit. Instead of being blue or red, it was purple, which is the mixture of both colors. I hadn't any idea what that meant and when I looked to Hyacinth, she looked just as perplexed. She shrugged her shoulders.

One of the guards at the tower leaned over and called down to us- "Everyone head to the main square! There will be an emergency forum there. Princess, your highness, you must go to the castle, it isn't safe for you to be about. I don't know what is happening, but protocol is to protect the royal family in these situations."

She was stubborn as usual. I told her I would accompany her in haste to the castle and make sure she was safe before I headed out alone to the forum. But she insisted on coming to the square and finding out what was going on alongside me. I couldn't argue. I couldn't convince her by arguing, and I hadn't the authority to force her to stay within the well protected stone castle surrounded by moat.

Nearly everyone in the kingdom was in attendance at the wide square. Some children were in the mermaid fountain, splashing about. Most wore looks of concern, but some were actually quite jovial. After all, the beacon fire wasn't red. It didn't mean there was danger afoot. Or did it? I didn't put it past the beacon guards to accidentally mix fire powders.

We waited an hour as the Order of Nine gathered on the platform to meet with the King and Syla. They were all on a dais, discussing something with great fervor. With them were some of the nobility, lords and ladies who were vociferously giving their twopence.

All eyes were on them as they bickered and politicked. They comprised the entire military hierarchy of the realm, meaning that what they were so forcefully deciding was a military action. The king, quiet for most of the hour, spoke precious few but decisive words. When the argument died down, it seemed a decision was made. The discussion was over, the king had spoken. Then they'd all settled down. A hush came over the audience. Brutus came forth, pushing a wheeled cart with a cloth over it to the center of the platform.

He began to speak to the now silent crowd. His voice was as strong as his back. "In light of the latest crimes against our realm by apparently magical creatures, the king and his order of knights tripled our security detail. My men and I patrolled the West Woods since we know that imps are forest-dwelling. We stalked and hunted, trying to find the creature. We put our best trackers sent hunting dogs about the wood, and for the longest time we found nothing.

"We had no way of smoking them out. Then I thought about

the fact that the creature or creatures, are essentially magical in nature. There are certain metals which have an effect on magic. Some creatures are affected by iron. Most are affected by silver. I went into town and found a blacksmith and a silversmith. I took a silver bell and an iron bell with me deep into the wood, alone. I rang them both over and over, hoping the sound would drive out the vile beast, causing it to reveal itself." He paused for effect. "And it did."

Hyacinth whispered in my ear as Brutus was talking. "He was one of my suitors, you know. He was bold, he was a resident for less than a month at the time. It was about a week before you arrived. Father hated him less than the ones before. In my mind, he was also too ambitious for the crown. I could read it in his beady eyes. There's something that doesn't sit well with me about him."

I nodded at her, cross-armed and wide eyed. Brutus has always struck me as odd. I reflected on how Sabrian reserved no judgment on the lower class and seemed to actually prefer them over the nobles. Then I brought my attention back to my lover's ex-suitor, who went on.

"It was an ugly thing that scurried about like a roach. It kept telling me to let it go, please let it go. I took an arrow from my quiver and bent back my bow as far as I could. 'Don't kill me! You'll be sorry!' It said. 'Let's make a deal, and avoid any bloodshed.' But you cannot bargain with a being of pure malice. I let my arrow fly, and it struck true, straight into the heart of the monster. And now all you faithful citizens, witness, and behold the foul stench of evil!"

He dramatically removed the cloth from the wheeled cart. The cart was made of wood. It was a small wooden cage with spoked wheels at the bottom, meant to carry small game.

Within it was a very small, very tiny red imp, which appeared even more red in the pool of its own blood. An arrow was lodged perfectly in the middle of its chest, almost too perfectly. It was almost as if it were expertly placed there after the imp died. Archers are rarely that good. But it could not have been falsified- the spilled blood proves that the arrow pierced where it did.

The people sucked in a collective breath. Most women and children hid their heads and turned away. Some cried, some ran away from the sight of it. Most of the men grew angry and demanded that more be done by the king. Their voices began to raise louder and louder until they drew together like drops of water forming a puddle.

"What do we do now??" many cried out.

"Where's my daughter? Where did the creature take it?" cried another.

"We must burn down the woods!" some said.

King Sabrian, stoic and in control, stood and raised his hands, palms facing the crowd. "My countrymen and women. There are some things we know and some things we don't. We don't know how this creature arrived in our land, or whether it's here alone. We don't know its intentions, why it did what it did, and what the repercussions will be from its clan, if it had any. It may have been lying when it said it was a prince, but that may have been factual.

"We don't know what it did with our children who went missing this time. I have every available man scouring the land for them. But whatever the answers to these questions may be, I want you all to know that we are going to be ever vigilant. The imp dared not show itself, dared not commit any of its heinous acts while our security level was high, but while our backs were turned it saw an opportunity to wreak havoc. My promise to you, is that our backs will never be turned again. Our patrols, guard, and lookout will be twofold all the time from here on in."

Just then, a very odd thing happened. I would scarcely have believed it had I not seen it happen myself. The body of the diminutive imp began to shake uncontrollably. It rattled immensely within the cage and then disappeared in a puff of red smoke, like a magic trick. The sound was like a pop from a wine cork. I'd opened many as a kitchen servant. The elite lords and ladies of the realm hold famously lavish parties.

We'd all looked at one another with fear and unknowing. I saw Haglinda and Al in the distance whispering to one another and holding hands as if nothing at all strange were happening. Al even stole a small kiss.

With my head turned, first looking afar and then to my side at my beautiful fiancee, I heard that wine cork popping sound again. Immediately in front of Sabrian there appeared a new puff of red smoke. When the wisps of scarlet cleared, there was a tall imp standing before the king. It held a parchment on a scroll and wore something akin to light mail armor.

The knights drew their swords and went to guard the king. The red imp bellowed out, "I come as a herald of the imp king, Erumite. I am here to officially inform you that the child you killed was a prince of Monello. We know he tried to beg for his life, but he was not spared. The young one intended to bargain with a member of your knighthood, but instead was slain on sight. What kind of monsters are you to kill a child?"

Sabrian looked afraid for the first time since I'd met him. I knew it was because he thought he was protected from magic like this. I remembered how Gatekeeper Al had told me the story about the attack that killed Queen Ophelia, and how before Sabrian exiled the witch in his court, she cast a powerful spell over the kingdom to keep it safe from magic intrusions.

King Sabrian regained his composure in a moment. He stood straight and looked positively regal. It was his responsibility and his burden to carry the weight of his people. His shoulders were well used to the weight. "That 'child' was over a century old. By our standards, he knew what he was doing when he provoked us. He maliciously destroyed our milk and food supply, kidnapped our children, and tormented our people. These are all provocative acts from your prince. As steward of my kingdom, I agree with the action my knight took in killing the demon."

The imp looked angry, but composed. He rolled up the parchment, apparently seeing that whatever was on it would not be listened to. As a herald, he seemed well versed in diplomacy, although he too was a creature of mischief.

"Did it not ever occur to you to use words rather than blades and arrows? Everything that imp child did could be undone. As a matter of fact, I have just reversed everything he did, personally. Your food and milk stores are replenished, and the 'kidnapped' children are returned to their parents. You forget that our magic comes from deception, and we can make things appear or disappear. Or appear as different than they truly are. The children weren't kidnapped, they were invisible and inaudible. These were harmless tricks, played by a harmless imp who knew no better. He may have only been testing his powers. You overreacted, and for that, there are serious consequences."

The king scoffed. "This realm has been attacked before with serious consequences. It is the right of every being to defend itself when it thinks it is being attacked. And with our history, we know the consequences of not acting swiftly enough. I reject your condemnation. But if it is any consolation, I am sorry your prince is dead. I shall send an official letter of condolence first thing tomorrow."

The herald re-scoffed and waved his hand dismissively. "It is not my purpose to debate or argue or comment on your feelings of sorrow. I come here bearing a message from King Erumite."

"Erumite?" Sabrian asked. "I heard you say his name just before but thought you must have been mistaken. Is it not Erubaca that rules the house of Monello?"

The herald looked genuinely dejected for a moment but regained his statesmanlike composure. "Not anymore. Erubaca abandoned his kingdom. I know you will not abandon yours. I come bearing conditions." He handed the rolled-up parchment to Brutus.

"In two days, our army will come to your door. You will either surrender your entire kingdom and all its possessions to Erumite, or be destroyed in battle. Those are your only two options. Erumite is furious. I will see you in exactly two days. You may summon me earlier if you wish. Simply say the words, 'I summon the herald of Monello' and I will appear to you." Then, he disappeared like his prince without so much as a farewell.

King Sabrian and his order of knights left the forum without saying another word. They strode to the castle and took Hyacinth with them post haste. Sabrian hadn't looked twice at me when he ripped her from my side. Randolph, on the other hand, looked at me with great import. There was gravity and solemnity in his eyes. He clapped my shoulder and rode off.

Dark times descend, I thought.

CHAPTER 4

I hadn't known how dark or how deep the trouble to come would be, but I knew it would be great. In this fight I must play a part, I decided. I would volunteer. The king and our people needed all the help they can get. I swore to contribute my blade and my mind towards the salvation of the kingdom. The governor of Mansfield who acts in the king's stead, directed the standing army to accompany the assembled citizens safely to their homes.

They tried to block the road to the castle but I told them I lived there as a servant. A lower level functionary told me to move along and that the castle was off-limits. I could not believe what I was hearing. "I am the king's personal baker! Let me through so I can volunteer my services as a fighter." I was irate, and hadn't known I could achieve that level of anger.

Since my "awakening" all I've ever felt was wonder, awe, appreciation and love from Hyacinth. As if her heart was the sun warming me into life, a welcome thaw after a long winter of forgetfulness. Like a tree might be brought to life in the sunny spring from a dark winter of death. Those kinder emotions were fading as worries and problems mounted one on top of another.

I began to walk up the gravel path but the low level function-ary pushed me back roughly. "I have me orders. And orders is orders. No one but the knights and the royal family may reach the castle. Sorry, mate. Find refuge in a pub somewhere if ye haven't a home."

I could not understand the level of irksomeness this man ra-diated. Nor why he was so far without reason. As if the only purpose to joining the guard was to push others with an author-ity he didn't actually possess. "But I live in the castle. I sleep in the castle. I have my own quarters! Let me through to the place where I live!"

He put his hand on my chest and pushed. "I've tried to be patient with ye, mate. Don't make me get back-up to escort ye to the castle but in chains and throw ye in the dungeon. B'cause I've got half a mind to."

"You've only got half a mind! I spoke to the king face to face just yesterday- we had breakfast together. I'm to marry his daughter, Princess Hyacinth, someday. You probably see her with me all the time. You will regret not letting me pass." It was the first threat I'd ever made, that I could recall. In retrospect, it was quite funny. I didn't know the chap's name nor did I have a plan of retribution.

He laughed with his hands on his hips. "If yer such mates, ye and the king, why ain't ye with them all makin' war plans right now? And if yer gonna marry the Princess like ye say, why is she safe and sound holed up in 'er room and ye're out here talkin' to me right now? Me, who's tellin' ya that ye can't pass this way? Bloody puzzlin', don't ye think?" He got me so angry that I must admit, I punched him right in his tin helmet.

Hyacinth was right- I was stronger than I looked. The work of a baker requires steady hands and quick wits. And the abil-ity to carry a hundred pounds of flour at a time. The fool fell to the floor, asleep. Unfortunately, his commanding officer and other guards in his company saw what I'd done and began to give chase. Apparently I was faster than I looked as well. I'd never galloped into a full run before but it was exhilarating. The fact that I was being chased by dim-witted guards added to my fun. They'd never catch me in their heavy uniforms.

However, the commotion I was making in my wake was not to go unnoticed. The newly doubled guardsmen all about took sight of me. There were several in front of me and to the sides. They'd swarmed around and were about to apprehend me. I didn't stand a chance, strong or not.

That is, if it weren't for Gatekeeper Al. His timing was impeccable. I'd stopped running and was about to taste a very severe rap on the head from the staff of a guard, when Al caught it in mid-blow. Everyone hushed. "Now listen here, ye guards are supposed to be the king's best. But ye aren't. Ye're bumbling fools, unable to see a problem when there is one, and unable to see a solution where there n'ain't one." I didn't know what he meant, nor did he perhaps, so I scratched my head as if I'd actually taken the blow.

He raised his chin to show superior authority. "I'm the Gatekeeper of this fair kingdom, and this here is the king's personal baker, Harold don't ye know. He'll also be yer king in twenty years at most I'd wager. He tried to tell ye that, didn't he? Now go off and be useful and keep yer eyes firmly peeled in case'n something actual happens."

They shuffled off, heaving threats at me impotently. "The nerve of the lot of them!" Haglinda, Al's wife, told me. "I'd put a hex on 'em if it weren't suspicious. And if we didn't need their beady eyes to keep us safe, that is."

"A hex?" I dusted myself off. "How can you hex them? You know how to wield magic?"

She looked at her husband Al in what I thought to be a very odd way. It was a quizzical expression. "No, lad. It's a manner of speaking. I didn't mean nothing by it." She looked me up and down as if she were a long-lost aunt, or some such relation. "Ya don't know who I am, do ye?"

I nodded gravely and took her hand once more to kiss it. "Gatekeeper Al's wife, my lady. We met a few weeks ago. You are a charming woman- how could I forget you?"

She looked at Al again with that same odd face. She spoke now without the slang and grammatical errors that mark the common person's speech in Mansfield. "And you? Do you know who you are yet? Don't you have questions about how you came here and the life you lived before?"

I didn't know what I looked like but I was sure my face was a question mark. "How did you know that I suffered from a lack of memory? I hadn't told anyone about it."

"Not even Hyacinth, your beloved." She laughed. "You both have a secret in common, I'm afraid. She doesn't remember how she came to be in the forest all those years ago, when Sabrian and Ophelia found her lost among the trees."

I squinted at them with newfound suspicion. I didn't know whether to further this conversation or to yell out for the guards. The strange knowledge possessed by Haglinda and Al might be impish in nature. They could be spies for the enemy. And yet there was a feeling in my bones that they were good people. There was a warm glow in them that could not be deceptive. "What are you both?"

They looked around to see if others were watching. Then they waved their hands over their faces. I assumed it was to reveal their true identities, and when they did, I almost screamed in fear. Their faces magically changed. Initially, I'd believed they were dead, but they were not. They were just very old- so old that the skin on their cheeks appeared to have melted, and the melted skin stuck to their skulls. If they were trying to frighten me, they succeeded. If they were trying to reassure me, they did not.

"The spell worked better than we thought it would, Harold." They restored their guises of Haglinda and Al, and I was never so happy to see such ugly faces in my life.

CHAPTER 4

Haglinda leaned close to my ear, fearing she'd be overheard. "I think your plans may have to be on hold, or even cancelled and I am truly sorry for that, my dear Harold. But this threat from Erumite is very real and very dangerous."

She pointed to Al and herself. "We have the power to defeat him, but only if we are revealed for the spellcasters we truly are. Not only that, but a military defeat of Erumite would leave the imps to break rank and run amok with no one to control. Even a defeat of Monello could become hazardous. Refugee imps under no obligation might enter and vex everyone in Mansfield with their tricks. You, above all, need to find a way to best them without war. You cannot let Sabrian fight. If he does, he will lose."

This strange woman who I now knew even less about must have been crazy. How could I possibly influence what the king will do?

"You're going to have to use cunning and trickery. A war is out of the question. Our magic would be too visible and there would be too many casualties. You will need to find another way. I hate to put this on you, seeing how all you've ever really wanted was a single iota of normalcy. You just wanted to enjoy being human and live out your days.

"But being human is all about facing these dangers in the twists and turns of your life's journey. There is no life without peril, from the smallest insect to the largest whale. Humanity is no different in that respect."

She was right. Now that the road was free, I needed to go to the castle and join the king's planning meeting. If I was ever to be a member of that world, I must take my opportunities when they present themselves. "Thank you Gatekeeper Al and Haglinda--"

"Those are not our real names," she said. She had a habit of nodding when she spoke. "You'll remember what they are soon enough. Now, you must do exactly what I tell you. Stay away from the castle for the time being. Head to the hill of the north lookout tower. Go where the moonlock bushes and grimmle-berry bushes grow together. Eat one grimmle-berry and you will remember everything. You're going to need that knowledge to help you. High Knight Randolph will meet you there, but you must hurry."

There was something solid in her conviction. I left them both and headed straight northward, although I didn't know what would greet me when I arrived. I was never sure that I wanted to remember my past since my present was so beautiful. And yet, I was compelled to follow the prophetic tidings of Haglinda. I feared, but I trusted her. I also trusted High Knight Randolph.

I knew him when he was Servant Randolph. How the mighty do rise! Who was I to question a witch...a witch? The only witch I'd heard of that was ever in Mansfield was Vanna. I paused. It was then that I realized that Vanna must be disguised as Haglinda. She never left Mansfield! If she was as powerful as what I'd heard Gatekeeper Al say...but Al is her husband. Of course he'd say she was powerful. Still, if she's half as powerful as I think, she's still able enough to defeat the horde of imps. I wondered at her reluctance, but I supposed I understood. Casualties determine the outcome of history.

Hyacinth, too, said she believed in other ways besides war. I'm not sure how it fell to me to discover them. I was a simple baker. But was I? I only remembered the past five months, which felt like five wonderful years. I decided that it was wrong of me to deny that I had a life before coming here. Although it was lost to me at that moment, finding it will prevent this war from happening and thwart the overthrow of the kingdom, according to Vanna.

I walked as quickly as I could. It was a cold day in mid-winter and I was not dressed for it. Every year people wish each other well in the dark months. "May you survive the winter" was a very common well-wish. People were saying it about town, except now they said it regarding the looming threat more than the cold. The cold, which was now bearing down on me fiercely. It would be almost an hour before I reached the hill. But it'd be shorter if I ran, I thought. So I ran. Straight uphill for fifteen minutes or so.

By the time I got to the northern hill I was as warm as an apple tart. And I was there in half the time. I warmed up and I arrived quickly, simply by willing my legs to move forward. For a moment I reflected on how resourceful a human mind can be. And yet, this resourceful mind could not decipher a solution or conjure a way out of this mess. The grimmle-berry and moon-lock bushes had a powdery covering of some light snow that fell as I was running.

Bending down to look at the plants, I thought about how very resourceful they too, must be. To be as plentiful as they are in this patch and yet be so rare elsewhere. To be able to survive the harsh winters. To even grow together without one killing the other. Truly these two marvels were the key to solving the problem. All I had to do was be like them.

Apparently a single berry would be all it took to recover my lost life. A life I hadn't known a thing about, not even its length. I assumed I was 27, but I could very well be 23. Or even 30 or more. I could almost be a grandfather if that were the case.

Did I want to know? I did not. How could learning about my past possibly help in this present endeavor? What is it about my past that would make me valuable? And if it was so wonder-ful, why did it abandon me? Or, perhaps it was I that abandoned it. I wouldn't know until I ate the grimmle-berry.

I plucked a bright red berry off its tiny branch. It was incred-ible that such a small thing could matter so much. I remember knowing that these fruits had amazing powers, but didn't recall everything that made them great. Rub it in your hand and the weak flesh can break. The skin practically falls off of it. Drop it and it splatters on the floor, since its flesh is weak. In a strange way these things were fragile. And yet to grow at all in such peril and through such harshness; to be so valuable, it must have an inherent virtue much greater than its weaknesses. Be like the berry, I told myself, taking a breath. Be greater than your weaknesses.

Closing my eyes, I ate the winter fruit, savoring the flavor of it. It was my favorite of all the berries. Grimmle-berry pie was my favorite pie after all. I waited a long moment and then opened my eyes, hoping to find that I suddenly knew all about my past. But all that happened was that my teeth rattled like playing dice in the overturned skull of a dead man. I was chattering uncontrollably. And I was expecting Randolph to be here. Hadn't the witch told me he would? Now that he was a High Knight, he was free to come when he pleased, apparently.

Nothing that the witch said would come to pass, happened. I was furious at her like I was about the pushy guard, except far more hungry and far colder. I was never so angry. I was about to turn tail and run back to the castle when a loud whisper caught my ear- "Erubaca!" I turned and saw no one. "Who's there?" I yelled. "I am Harold Baker- who are you?"

"Erubaca!" The voice was louder and it seemed to come from everywhere all at once. Every direction echoed its vibrations. "Erubaca!" It became louder and closer. There was no one near me at all. The hill was clear- there was no cover. No one could be close enough to make that sound and not be seen. "Erubaca, Erubaca, ERUBACA!" It seemed like the loudest explosion from the greatest volcano, except it came from within me.

My head splintered like a dry rotten plank of wood and I drunkenly fell to my knees. The world spun through me in a tumble and a great nausea overcame me. After regurgitating what little food was in my belly, I felt much better. Wiping my mouth I thought, "Oh no. I remember now. I remember...everything." I began to weep. This was a difficult riddle to solve, and there was no way for me to win, even if I could prevent a war. I would lose everything either way.

Either I deceive my brother and lose my humanity, or I remain human and see Mansfield fall. That was my home now, and humanity was my shroud.

My brother was making my former kingdom hostile. With my departure, in a way it was his to rule however he pleased. He was next in line after all. But I hadn't given him the full legitimacy of that position. I didn't give him the binding talisman, the ring, that would have given him the right to govern.

Maybe that's what he's after, I thought. Maybe he thinks that Sabrian's royal archives have some spell book or reference that will help him find it. Good luck. I didn't even know where it was after I handed it to Vanna. And I had full trust in Vanna's abilities to hide it. If she wanted it gone, then it would never be found.

Magic kingdoms are not like human ones. They don't actually require a ruler, but usually there is one as a figurehead. It's the reason I didn't mind leaving in the first place. Imps are creatures of instinct, ruled by their own inner desires. For the most part, they can keep themselves in check. They naturally follow mischief and prefer not to let it lead to malice. They don't need a government to provide for them or protect them. They don't usually follow orders except those given by people they fear. Or by the possessor of the talisman. The only legitimacy is power.

I looked down at my hands. Human. Calloused. My hands crept up to my face and I felt for my beard like a blind man attempting to recognize a stranger. These hands no longer had power. I had the memory of a thousand years but the strength of 30. There was no winning. I would lose Hyacinth in every direction I walked. If I threw in my skill as a master deceiver and it worked, then the spell would be broken, because deception is supposed to "become me not." I'd become Erubaca again, except lost with no home.

If I fought alongside the humans in battle I would lose. I'd either die or be defeated, because there was no way a human army could truly defeat a magical one head-on, without the assistance of magic. Hyacinth would be disappointed I didn't try another way. But what other way?

If I simply walked away and abandoned Mansfield, I'd be lost without a compass or a bearing, or a light in the world. That would not be a life I had wanted to live. I would not be subject to my brother's invasion. I would not serve him. What I had to do was focus on my brother. What were his weaknesses?

Now I heard footsteps in the snow, gently crushing the light powder with each stomp of a boot. I looked up. It was Randolph! No, not Randolph. It was Radegast! Randolph was Radegast in costume, the entire time I was in Mansfield and I hadn't recognized him. To be fair however, five months ago I couldn't recognize my own reflection.

"Radegast!" I blurted.

"Shh!" he yelled back, hands pushing the air. "So you remember who you are. Good. I am to spirit you away secretly to the king. The Order of Nine and the House of Nobles have voted to wage war, I'm afraid. The ultimate decision is with Sabrian and Syla, but the Order's decision holds grave weight. Brutus was the most vocal about it."

"I don't much like Brutus, Radegast, if I'm to be honest."

Radegast, who looked somewhat different from when I first met him, smiled slyly. His eyes were not silver any longer. I didn't know if Vanna did this or if he himself could- he was a form shifter after all. "He is one of your own, Harold. I see others as they truly are, remember. Of course, I see others as they believe they are, too. And as others see them. It's difficult to describe, but I have triple-vision when I look at any living creatures."

One of my own? Indeed. "Who is he? Is he my brother? Has he been here the entire time?"

Radegast shook his head. His resemblance to a wolf was un-canny, now that I remembered him. "He is an imp spy, one who is in league with your brother. He's the fellow you met on your journey to see Vanna. Before you met me."

"Apple-Eater!"

"Yes and he's been here since little before I arrived. After you went into hibernation from the honey golden tea she gave you, Vanna foretold of a great danger to Mansfield. She found me in the forest and asked me to come here and do what I could to protect it. She told me about you, that you would be the one to save the people. You would find a way. That's what she said back then.

"Now tonight, I spoke to the king after the Order of Nine retired and told him I myself had a vision, that Vanna named you by name to be our salvation. I said that she gave me a dire warning not to engage in battle and to have faith in you. He knew Vanna very well years ago but does not know that she still watches over him. He trusts her. He will give you his ear."

"But I don't know what to tell him!" I paced in the snow with my hands firmly pressed into my sides. "Why did Apple-Eater make believe he was loyal to the kingdom? If Erumite wanted Mansfield to be crushed so he could have access to the royal archives, couldn't he have let the dragons do their worst instead of slaying them?"

Radegast, who was well draped in a blue cowl, almost coughed in laughter. "There were no dragons. They were con-jured-up illusions, intended to strike fear and awe in everyone present. Knowing this, and knowing that Brutus wanted to be elevated by his heroics, I jumped into the false fire along with him. I knew the fire wouldn't hurt me and that I wasn't in real danger. Yet Brutus didn't know that I doubted him- he thought I was fooled like the rest of them. I must say, the illusions were very intricate."

That was brilliant. It would make Brutus seem courageous,

and his faithful allegiance to the realm would be unquestioned. His position as High Knight could have, in his mind, given him access to the archives. But Sabrian denied him access- only Sabrian may protect them and at either rate the archives are enchanted. One thing I know about Erumite is his impatience, so he invented a reason to invade- the death of an imp "prince" who no doubt was also an illusion.

"The enemy is clever, very clever," Radegast concluded. "But although they are clever, Vanna and I are clever too. They do not suspect we are all here, trying to foil them. I'm beyond reproach, such 'pals' as Brutus and I are. He is so desperate for a friend. In the end, all he wants is to belong, anywhere that will accept him and appreciate him."

I nodded. Apple-Eater and Erumite were indeed clever. To start a confrontation under false pretenses, and give the humans the impression that they were the ones that had committed the wrong. "They fooled me," I said. Then my eyes opened, both literally and figuratively. I am easily fooled. I might be human now but for a thousand years my nature was elseways. My former kind is good at deception and yet are easily deceived themselves. Erumite's strength is also his greatest weakness. He is an imp.

Before leaving, there were a few things irking me that I decided to ask my friend. One was how these magical creatures seem to come and go from here as they please? Was there not a magic-sniffing dog at the gate? Radegast reminded me that the dog belonged to Gatekeeper Al, and that Gatekeeper Al was Warlocke. And that magic doesn't smell like anything in particular anyway.

Was there not an enchantment surrounding the place I wondered aloud? Since Apple-Eater was able to enter without being caught the first time, it negated the effect of the protection spell. It did not fully negate it, however. There was still a basic protection from harm, although the barrier was far weakened. The hex surrounding the archives too, held strong but were made somewhat flimsier by Apple-Eater's undetected arrival. Yet the only thing that could allow Erumite entry to them was the official hand-off of power from the house of Sabrian.

The other question was about my true form. "Since you see the true form of others, please tell me, I beg you. What do you see when you look at me? And what of Hyacinth? What is the nature we possess?"

Radegast stood tall and firm, and gently shook his head. He would not tell me. I would not want to know, or it would not help me to know. Whether human or otherwise, it did not matter. In the short time I was human I'd seen many people seek validation, and in fact identity, through the mirror of others. I supposed I was doing the same thing now.

"Let's go," I told the werewolf, rubbing my shoulders. "I'm freezing." We began to move along when Radegast perked up. His ears actually inclined like those of a fox, alert that there may be rabbits about. He raised his hands for me to hush and stop walking. "What is it?" I asked.

He whispered, "It's Brutus with some of his men. It sounds like they are looking for me. They're fetching me for a special meeting of the Order to draw up battle plans in case Sabrian declares war. They can't find me talking to you. It's too suspicious."

"How far are they?" I asked.

"Close. It's alright if they find you here alone. Tell them you came out for the brisk air, that it helps bring you clarity. And go back with them. I'm going to transform into a wolf and head back to the castle of my own accord. I'll be back waiting for them when they get back."

His face began to change as if he were a snarling animal. He growled. I heard a rumble like that of thunder, and in fact the sky directly above us became menacingly dark. There were some flashes of lightning and a thunderclap. When I looked back at Radegast he was a tremendous black wolf running towards the forest faster than any deer I'd ever seen. He would never go hungry if he remained in that form.

About the time I saw him disappear from view, Brutus in full High Knight regalia came wandering by himself over the cusp of the hill. "Ho there," I called out. Brutus looked more than surprised.

"Ho," he said. "What brings you here, Harold? This is a usually desolate hillside. And at the moment it's also quite cold. Only the devil would come out on a night like this dressed like you."

I didn't need to explain myself to a former subject of mine. But I did. "I come here often to seek solace and find inspiration." I looked at the moonlock and grimmle-berry bushes, intertwined, mortal enemies at each other's borders yet thriving together. Then, to subtly remind him I was the one of us who wound up with the princess, "As you know, Hyacinth and I come here every morning at daybreak to greet the world with the new sun. It is so different at night. Nothing to greet. Only to mourn." I was a sad singer, distracting him from his thoughts.

He looked about without interest. "Yes, I guess so. Would you like an escort back to Mansfield Castle? My men and I are on our way back."

Poor Apple-Eater. He has a good soul, I thought. Albeit wayward. He only followed the directives of my brother because as Radegast noticed, he wants a place to belong. He wants approval and friendship. It's not condemnable. It's a universal desire. "I've always liked you, Brutus," I said. "I never got a chance to properly congratulate you on your victory over the dragons. I am honored to have such a noble, trustworthy knight defending my homeland. May you always stand with the great ones."

He was taken aback with the weight of my kind words. I am practiced in the art of deception, and I know when it is working. This however was sincere on my part. And it was working. When we returned to the castle, Radegast that is, Randolph, greeted us at the main door. "It is late, Brother Brutus. We need all nine to be together in order to call our planning meeting into session. Nine is quorum, you know. Hello Harold, how are you this fine evening?"

Brutus eyed him sideways. "Yes, I came out looking for you, Randolph."

"Well it looks like you've found me." He clapped us on our shoulders in a friendly welcoming way.

"Indeed." Brutus and I entered. His men wandered off to their posts. Randolph expertly whisked away his pal to the War Room, which was located sufficiently far from the king's quarters and his archives.

I headed there straightaways. When I got to the top floor of the castle, I saw a torchlight glowing outside Sabrian's chambers. Sabrian and Syla were discussing plans with great furor. I decided to listen a bit before I went in. "We need to attack Monello outright! Let us go there under the cover of darkness. We must surprise them with overwhelming might- that is our only chance at victory!" Syla was practically raving. I heard her hit the stone wall with her fist. I believe it hurt the wall more than it hurt her.

"Sweetheart, please calm down. What you suggest is too passionate to be the right course of action. We can't afford to tie up our entire army in a surprise attack against a race of creature we know little about. They have profound magical ability. Plus, we don't even know where Monello is or how to get there." His voice was even and tempered, like forged steel. I heard him turning the pages of a book calmly.

"What about what little magic we have left? Father, what about all the studying you do every night in that damned room?" Her voice sounded like the roar of a bear.

"It's useless, Syla. I have no gift for it. No mind, no heart or soul for what magic entails. I could barely light kindling with all the magic knowledge I possess. I can't learn what needs to be known. It's too difficult for me." I heard him throw a heavy book onto a table. "I shall go retire for the evening. We shall speak in the morning."

"I'm sorry Lord Sabrian for delaying your sleep, but we should speak now," I said as I entered the room gravely. The two royals appeared startled. "Forgive me for my boldness, but we must act to outwit our foes rather than fight them. There is no conquest in power. If we fight, we cannot win."

Syla, who appeared sincere yet frustrated, barked, "And what do you know? Why does a witch who hasn't been here in years have anything to do with our decisions on such matters? Who is she to tell us what course of action to take?" She was tying her boot laces together and seemed to be getting ready to invade Monella all by herself. Her armor, daggers, shield and sword were splayed out on the floor. There was even a slingshot.

Thankfully, the grimmle-berry brought back my gift of persuasion. "Randolph, in whom you have full faith when it comes to matters of knighthood, had a vision, did he not? You trust him to defend your realm, so trust his instincts. He believes in me. I don't know why I was named by the witch. To be honest, I am reluctant to play this part. But I accept it if it means I can help. And I will do it for all the reasons you'd want me to, but mostly for Hyacinth." I looked at Syla as profoundly as I could. "I love her deeply." I pulled up a heavy wooden chair and sat down among them. I would not be dismissed.

I looked at the both of them with unwavering eyes. One must convey a sense of seriousness even though they are playing a trick. To sell the product at any cost, that is the thing. The greatest mischief-makers are not just artisan craftsmen but also vendors. Syla's fire was burning brightly. Sabrian was tired and resigned. His fire was a candle in a blizzard. Constant worry and constant vigilance will do that over a lifetime.

I looked at the king. "Though loved ones may leave you, and friends betray you, your scars will never leave you as long as you live. But try not to find solace in that, my lord. For it is the propensity of old scars to seek the company and comfort of new scars that I find most troubling."

"Is that a threat, Baker?" Sabrian had found his roar as well. He stood up. It was a tactic to demonstrate a distinct size advantage.

I remained seated. "No my King, merely a warning. You trusted Vanna and still do. Though you exiled her out of fear, she continues to fight for you and watch over your people. If you trust her, trust me. She believes I am the only one capable of defeating Erumite. And I have a plan."

"What do you need from me?"

"Let me into your archives."

CHAPTER 5

After milling through the archives with King Sabrian's watchful but inattentive eyes on me, I thanked him and then spirited off to Hyacinth's chambers. I found her torchlight spent and it was very difficult to navigate through the pale moon wisps in the darkness.

Arriving at her chambers, I found her frozen, fixated on the window through which she was looking. It was as if she were trying to divine the future from the ghostly dim trail of moonlight that entered her room. "Sweetheart," I whispered trying not to startle her.

Without taking her eyes off the starlit sky, ablaze with the glory of numberless suns, she said, "I was sending a very strong intention to the universe that I would see you soon. I was hoping past hope that you'd come to me tonight, my love." She turned to me. "There is much sadness coming. I can sense it in the wind. It is colder than it feels. For some reason, this truth is open to me."

"Yes," I said. "There is sadness coming. But mostly for us." Hyacinth took my hand and found that I was wearing gloves.

"You're all dressed to go out, Harold," she said as a matter of fact. She squeezed my hands.

"I want you to forgive me, my love," I nearly cried. My voice quaked like the echoes of a choir lamenting a funeral dirge in a large cathedral. "No matter what I do next, I will lose you. But what I do will prevent a slaughter. I'm going to Monello now to speak to the King of the Imps."

She grabbed me by the arms and pulled me towards her with all her strength. With strength greater than her own she embraced me. "What will you do there? You won't do anything foolish, will you? Something that will get you killed?"

I embraced her filled with the same love and fear. "No. I have found another way."

I left the castle and noted how little security there was about. Since all the guards were stationed throughout the country, there were less left to defend the castle proper. This fact allowed me to "borrow" a horse, as we would sometimes do in the mornings. I decided to take Mayberry on this quest. What I was about to do I needed to do quickly and under the cover of darkness. She was a fine mount.

I'd taken the horse to the northern hill, off to the eastern side which grows moonlock and grimmle-berries together. The northern lookout tower is big and the view from there is vast, but the guards posted there could not see everything. In fact, unless someone came bearing a torch, it would be hard to see anyone at all in the blackness of night. In any case, I was known to most of the northern guards as someone who often comes to the hillside, even though I was usually accompanied by royalty.

I bent down to the ground and plucked what I needed off the bush. You're pulling off one of the greatest scams of your life, I thought. Perhaps the greatest. All the wheels were in motion. "I summon the herald of Monello" I spoke to the wind. In a moment I saw a puff of red before me. I coughed. The smoke was unnecessary.

When the air cleared, the same messenger began, "Very good.

I was hoping your decision would be quick, King Sabrian-- wait, you're not the king." To be fair, I am the king. But I allowed him to go on. He looked around. "Where is the king? And where are we? What desolate, sad place is this?" For an imp, he was far too uptight. He lived to serve, not to mislead or have any fun. He was not my herald, so must have been given his position by Erumite, whom he wished to impress.

I maintained an even tone and whisper, although shouting would have sufficed. "I would like to speak to your master," I said as humbly as I could. "I come with an offer, not from the king, but an offer to pull the greatest trick against the humans Erumite has ever pulled. I know he is instigating a war for ulterior motives. He wishes access to the king's archives."

The imp seemed truly upset by my words. He appeared insulted. With gray eyes ablaze, he huffed "How dare you accuse the Imp King of such treachery?" It was a laughable question. Treachery was Erumite's middle name. That or Gerald, I forget which. The imp's acting could use a bit of refinement, I thought. He oversold it. "I am leaving now. There is no reason for me to stay here any longer and listen to you; you are not the representative for your kingdom."

"And neither are you," I told him flatly. From my well-concealing cloak, I pulled out a beautiful sword. He seemed unsure of what he should do or what my motives were, so he waited. Biding time is a good ploy, one I've used countless times. "It is the Clamoring Blade, herald. I stole it. I have been to the royal archives. I have discovered a better way of winning against the humans that does not involve shedding blood. That after all, is not the imp way." I would know the imp way.

He hesitated, and was about to refuse me. You must interrupt a refusal before it begins, if you ever have a hope of overcoming it. I raised the sword and handed it to him. "This is a token of my allegiance with Monello. I am proving to you that I am a traitor to Mansfield. King Sabrian let me into his archives

119

because I claimed to know magic and that I would be an asset in the upcoming war. You see, Sabrian himself is terrible at magic, and so the information he has at his disposal does him no good against you."

The herald held the blade in his hand, and could have struck me down then and there and put an end to it. But imps would rather trick you into suicide than killing you outright. My brother was a big lover of intricate plots. And the one I was about to deliver was as intricate as he'd seen.

"Come," the herald said. He transported us both in a whirlwind of red directly to Erumite, who was stationed with a company of imp soldiers some miles away from Mansfield. Imp soldiers were nearly impossible to control. The young ones always wanted to play, and the old ones were hard pressed to do anything other than philosophize about their tricks. Yet, Erumite seemed to have them all well behaved.

A group of about a hundred of them were in very funny war gear. To see an imp in a suit of light armor, bearing a sword and shield is fairly strange to me. But none of them was out of character. They sat around a small fire in silence, with Erumite posted on a rock, his eyes on the walled kingdom of Mansfield in the distance. He could only guess what was happening there, since the telescope had not yet been invented.

When imps are about to see a plan come to fruition, they have a heightened sense of purpose. This could be why they seemed to be so serious. But that also meant it would be difficult to change plans on them. Difficult. Not impossible.

"My lord," the herald spoke. "I have brought you here a citizen of Monello who says he was just in the archives. He wishes to betray his people and help us."

Erumite was not a good person. At any point of his life. "I don't need his help. One way or another, Mansfield is going to be ours. Take him back to his home and seal his mouth shut so he can tell no one where he's been."

120

CHAPTER 5

Before the herald could reply with, "Very good, sir," I stated loudly so the rest of the men could hear, "King Erumite, the Order of Nine and the House of Nobles have voted to declare war on Monello. All that's needed is Sabrian's word and you will be drawn into a fight. In this fight, you would certainly win. But Mansfield is well armed and has the finest human military in the world. You would lose soldiers for certain."

I spoke those last words the most loudly. If there's one thing imps hate, it's dying. Erumite looked over to his men. They'd heard me. So I decided to continue. "My name is Harold. I am the king's baker and also suitor to his daughter, so I may speak frankly to the king. He is very fond of me. I told him I knew magic, which I do not. It was a lie.

"I convinced him to let me into his archives, to find a way we could make peace with Monello and avoid death. On both sides. He agreed to suspend a decision on making a declaration of war until I spoke with you. You may think of me as his secret emissary. And yet what I bring to you is more than what the Mansfield king thinks. If it means no loss of life, I pledge you my allegiance and the betrayal of my people."

He motioned to me to follow him away from the soldiers. "I'm listening. What do you have to offer? And what are you trying to get at, what do you get in all of this? There is no good reason to come directly to your king's enemy, who can kill you with but a look."

Erumite appreciated overtures from humans, so I bent low to show him respect. Most imps didn't care about things like that, but my brother did. "Lord Erumite, I am in love with the king's daughter Hyacinth. She is my world. Anything and everything I can do to spare her and her family, I would be willing to do."

Erumite played the part of the benevolent warlord. "Love is a great motivator for your kind. What is it you suggest? Bear in mind, the decision is mine alone." He clicked his tongue in thought.

"I suggest you sign a peace treaty with Mansfield for one hundred years."

Erumite laughed as if to call me a fool. "Why would I do that, young Harold Baker?"

"To play the greatest trick of your life, of course." An imp, especially this one, would find it hard to resist outdoing himself. Bigger and better is the best way. The only way. I reached into my jacket pocket and pulled out a few leaves to show him. I could tell he was intrigued. You must be able convince your mark if you intend to manipulate him.

I lifted the leaves up to his nose. "It's moonlock, a very potent leaf that grows from a rare plant. It grows only on one side of the north hill of Mansfield."

My brother's eyes raised. He hadn't ever heard of it. "It's a poison?"

I handed it to him. "Of sorts. It has an immediate effect on humans and a delayed effect on magical creatures, like you. A small amount will cause the person who ingests it to sleep. For a hun-"

"A hundred years..." his voice trailed off as he looked towards Mansfield. He saw where I was trying to lead him.

I nodded. "You wake up as if you slept but a night, refreshed and renewed as if nothing had happened at all. Sign a treaty that expires in one hundred years- that way everyone sleeps right through it and when they awaken they must surrender. That way, no one can dispute it, and no one dies.

"Now, it is a custom for peace treaties to be accentuated by the peace toast, where the two sides drink either ale or tea. It would fall to me and the king's kitchen staff to boil the tea or serve the ale at the event. The custom states that all members, that is the entire kingdom of both signing parties, must drink the toast. It is a superstition, but one that Mansfield takes very seriously.

"I say you make the peace, sign the treaty to reign in a century of tranquility between Monello and Mansfield in front of the entire crowd. I will put moonlock in the grand batch of tarot root tea to be served. Everyone will sleep through the length of peace-time. In a century when they wake, the treaty is null, and they must concede defeat. Then the archives are yours without a single red drop fallen. A century for an imp is a long nap, is it not?"

He kept rolling the spiky leaf over in his hands. "Something so small can do so much?" It was not a question really, merely a statement of some fact that was difficult for him to believe.

I nodded and smiled. I'd gotten through to him. I handed him something else now, a small parchment that I ripped from a book in the archives. It described moonlock and had an illustration of the leaf so he could verify what I was saying. I gave it to him to further his trust in me.

"Sometimes the smallest is the greatest. As for me, I will drink tea from another batch of untainted tarot root. When all of Mansfield is asleep, I shall take as much king's gold as I can carry and be on my way. I am something of a nomad so I will find no trouble drifting from place to place. Oh, and your army being magical, you will have enough time to return to Monello before the moonlock takes effect. It has a delayed impact on your kind."

Erumite was fairly familiar with human motivations. You must be properly acquainted with them in order to exploit them. Among them all, love and money are perhaps the greatest, so there was no reason for him to doubt me.

I continued. "My people will not surrender. It is either a hard fought win with many casualties, or this clever ploy which are the two options at your mighty disposal, my lord. It is my humble opinion that you should take the second option. It provides you the opportunity to do the greatest mischief. This way no one loses, and you are the biggest winner. "

My brother beamed as if he'd thought of it himself. He

handed back the leaf proudly. I knew that if he if didn't need me to spike the tea, he'd have done away with me, such was the darkness that resided in him. "Make it so, Baker. But heed my warning young fleshling, if you betray me in any way I will rain a world of torment upon you. Death would be the only escape from your very own personal tragedy, do you understand me?"

His threat was a test. Humans react different ways when they are lying and when they tell the truth. So I sought to prove I was telling the truth. "Though I be a lowly laborer, you yourself have seen how cunning I can be. Had I wanted anything other than what I've told you, I could have had it. I could have poisoned the leaf I handed you, or slew you with the Clamoring Blade that instead I give you as a gift. As a token of my sincerity.

"Instead of coming to you I could have used this opportunity to run away from Mansfield and all these problems but instead I stay to speak to the great King of the Imps. To beseech your wisdom. For love. And a little bit of money. But maybe I should withdraw my invitation to help you and see how many imps fall before it's all over." I breathed the heavy breath of a just man, questioned of integrity.

His red eyes and gray face contorted. He was mulling it over. "That is not necessary. We will do it your way. I will send my herald back with you to declare that a hundred year peace has been brokered. A deal has been struck. I will not tell my men of the moonlock. I will tell them only that we have made new allies. I'll let them know we will not fight our new friends. That should make them happy at any rate. They are mostly young and friend-making is a highly sought thing for them." It played out well.

He called for the herald and gave him news of our diplomacy. The herald and I then returned to Mansfield in triumph, again through billowing red smoke. Sabrian and Syla were awake and waiting for news. Hyacinth and most of the kingdom was asleep, their cares detached from them, floating just above their heads till they return to wakefulness.

124

CHAPTER 5

Sabrian embraced me when I relayed the information. Syla remained recalcitrant. She didn't trust any enemies of her house. Nor had she trusted my motives for brokering such a deal. She never hated me, but she never liked me either. Her arms remained folded throughout the informal peace talk between Sabrian and the herald.

The herald, completely bland, expressed his congratulations and thanks. He alerted us all that rather than an invasion, they should expect the house of Monello to visit in two days' time, to sign a treaty between the realms that would last an entire century. I interjected that I would be more than happy to serve my famous tarot root tea as the peace toast drink. My offer was accepted graciously by both of them.

When I was an imp, I never traveled via puff of smoke, but my new friend seemed enthralled by it. After Erumite's herald left, Sabrian shook my hand with the strength of many vicegrips. It was weary and yet like tempered iron. He patted my shoulder in appreciation and retired to his bedchamber. Before leaving he told me, "I won't awaken anyone tonight. There will be an official announcement tomorrow. For now, let those asleep keep sleeping, and those keeping vigil continue to remain vigilant."

Syla lingered in the room, which was part War Room, part armory, part study, part lounge. Her arms still folded, she told me, "This had better not be some kind of game, for you or them, or anyone. This peace of yours had better work itself out. Or I will be there to rip the throats of all that seek the destruction of my house." She looked into my eyes, as if she were Radegast peering into my soul to find the truth. "No matter how close. I saw my mother killed when I was a child. Never again will I allow anything like that to happen. Never again." She walked away with grave purpose.

Sleep suddenly falling upon me, contending with my eyelids, I wanted to see Hyacinth once more. I wandered to her quarters like a stumbling drunk. She was soundly adream.   Her eyes fluttered like butterfly's wings in the dew of morning. I breathed deeply and then sighed.

Although the inheritance of the king was to fall upon her head, I noted how fair her constitution was, how weak the neck meant to bear that crown. And she, asleep in the face of darkest danger, always a voice of peace even when war is necessary. She would be no queen and I, no king. My former crown should never have been given me. I was no Sabrian. But I needn't have been.

I lay myself sprawled upon the divan in her chamber. I rolled a blanket upon me, and then let myself be swept into a welcome oblivion, where danger was as far away from me as my ability to perceive it.

CHAPTER 6

I awoke to my love stealing kisses from me. Groggily, I informed her, "You don't need to steal them, they're free." She beamed back at me. She must have heard the news that I single-handedly avoided a catastrophe. How little she knew of what I really did. In time I hoped she'd forgive me, and come to understand why I did what I did. Why there was no other way. Sometimes there are no good options, only less bad ones.

I held her face in my right hand. She kissed my fingers as she inclined into my hand. "You saved us. Apparently you have a power of persuasion greater than any sword can affect. I am so proud of you." How innocent, to think that peace comes without a price. I arose slowly and told her I had to get breakfast started.

"No, you must be at the town square when my father announces the good news. You were the emissary that achieved the pact we are about to enjoy. You are the man of the hour. When the agreed upon peace expires, we will all be long dead."

I shook my head at her as I went to put on my pantaloons. "I spoke to your father last night. I want him to get credit for the deal-making. Sometimes the leader of the land needs something to legitimize their power, especially when their position is a difficult one. There are so many detractors and nay-sayers, and alternate opinions that a leader's voice must always vie to be the loudest. In the future, your father will be unquestioned when he makes a decision."

She looked puzzled. She hadn't thought that this treaty was not the end of all problems, and that Mansfield is still in a highly volatile place in the world. "You won't even be present as the King speaks?"

I shook my head again. "No. May humility serve me better in the shadows than in the light, now and always. The people don't know me yet. They know Sabrian. And Syla. And you. You must be there today, and every day. You too, must legitimize yourself as the future Queen. Not here and there when it suits you, but always." It may have been harsh. I kissed her upon the lips and squeezed her hands. "I shall ride to the northern hill alone this morning. There is much that weighs heavily on my heart. You should probably think about speaking a few words after your father. Please think them through. Prepare this great land for a feast of thanksgiving and calm, and better days ahead. Lead, and they will follow."

Hyacinth was obviously confused. I hadn't ever asked anything of her before, only to be herself. Unencumbered by anything else. But love must sometimes make demands, and love must also heed them. "Yes I will, Harold. Be safe. And thank you again." She curtsied as if in respect. I could detect some sadness from her as she struggled to understand why I was acting so strangely.

I departed from her again. It seems I am always departing from her lately and claiming it is for her sake, but it is. I rode the horse I always steal from the knights' stables to the hill. Mayberry was well acquainted with me. The darkness was still drenching the horizon, but sunlight was slowly pouring in, both mixing together a strange brew.

Under the cover of dying darkness, I bent to collect all the items I needed for the brew of my own. I put everything in my satchel before the dawn could bring my unauthorized harvest to light. I lingered a while to look at the majesty of creation. The endless horizon brings to mind an endless existence, but full of both light and darkness in equal measure.

It wasn't often that I doubted myself. One thing I would never doubt however, was that I made a great decision to becomes human in the first place. As an imp I would have looked at a sunrise, but I would not have seen it.

I heard a sounding of the Great Horn come distantly from the south. It was answered by the north just a few stadium lengths from me. The light of the beacon burned blue, of course. And all the king's men were telling the people to go to the square. Everything was like clockwork. It was like the movements of the kingdom were the movements of the grass blades in the wind, touched by the whims of alternating night and day. Firmly rooted, but swayed this way and that.

Within a half hour, the king would begin his speech to reassure the entire populace that the cruel twists of the past month were over. A new era would be ushered in of mutual stability and dare he even say it? Trust between the demonspawn and themselves. But you can't exactly trust a creature whose sole purpose it is to exploit that trust. And it isn't their fault. As a former one of them I know, it was not in my power to be other than what I was or do other than what I did. What it took for me to change was not an epiphany of some grand truth, but a weariness within myself.

I told myself that if I left now, I could reach the square in time to see Hyacinth speak. So I went. But I reminded myself that I mustn't be seen by her. Her role as leader of this land must not be sullied by a love that cannot be, despite my best efforts.

When I arrived, horse-less since I'd put Mayberry away in her rightful home, I saw Hyacinth receive the floor from her father with grace. There was a majesty and an importance to the way she held herself. It outshone the morning that I earlier witnessed rising from the dead.

There was always greatness inside of her, but she hadn't always known it. And I could tell she didn't know it now. Not fully. She addressed the people in a loud booming voice,

"My friends! Rejoice that we may all welcome enemies turned allies to our fair land on the morrow. We shall celebrate renewed faith in our neighbors and in our own might. Faith in our ability to establish relations with others and to effect the greater world around us. We must be proud and also thankful for the warriors in our midst, especially the warriors for peace. Pacifism is strength, not weakness, and both sides have shown considerable strength.

"Join me in marking this most happy occasion with the peace toast tomorrow! It is customary, not to mention good luck, for all members of the house of Monello and that of Mansfield to drink the draught. I promise it will be momentous and delicious. I will be assisting my betrothed, someone very instrumental in the peace deal, Harold Baker, in brewing it. Now a server, someday a king." She turned to me and smiled. She saw me, as always. She turned back to the crowd. "Bring your appetite, your thirst, and your love of country with you tomorrow as we celebrate with the greatest feast of our time!"

This certainly was a land of many feasts. And I had my secret ingredient well secured in my satchel. Therefore I allowed myself respite for a day. After the forum that followed the announcement, which I didn't pay much attention to, I found Hyacinth chatting with some nobles. A lord here, a lady there. Pompous fools with hands unworn, whose vote counts as much as that of the knights. She needed to interact with them and be known in order to secure their backing when the day comes to be crowned.

Before I could reach her, Vanna, that is Haglinda, accosted me. Warlocke, that is Gatekeeper Al, interjected himself into Hyacinth's conversation before her attention could turn to me.

He distracted her while Vanna approached me. "Hello, Harold," Haglinda said. She was smiling, so I knew she was happy with the way things were turning out. Unless the expression I saw was queasiness, nausea, or some kind of witchy disappointment.

She spoke far too loudly for my comfort. "Is everything in place for tomorrow? It looks like Erumite took the bait. You did a good job selling peace. Did you give him the Blade?" I nodded. "The Clamoring Blade can be used only once. Then it is only a regular sword," she informed me, loudly. "So it's a good thing it's useless." I nodded again, looking around. Why was she speaking so freely in front of potential interlopers?

"What did he say when you showed him the parchment describing the moonlock? And is he alright with drinking it himself, he and his men? Speak up now."

"Yes, ma'am," I whispered. "He would rather sleep through a hundred years than stay awake pining for the ring. As of now, the moonlock is a secret only he knows. His men also think a peace has been reached."

"Did you collect all that you need yet? Now the rest is squarely up to you." She looked around surreptitiously. I inclined my head to my satchel and nodded. She seemed to find what, or who she was looking for. "Radegast has some news you should hear." She waved him over. Randolph quickly joined our now trio after shaking the hand of a duke to wrap up a meaningless conversation. My eyes went to Hyacinth, where they met hers. Gatekeeper Al was speaking to her quickly and loudly about being a young man in the knighthood when Sabrian was born. It was all fluff, intended to stall her.

Randoph, Haglinda and I were huddled up together. He embraced me with pride. "Vanna has enchanted our conversation. No one can understand what we are saying, no matter how inclined they are to listen or loud we speak." That answered a lot of questions. "From my end, there seems to be one small flaw. Brutus is beside himself. He is suspicious of everything,

I can see it in him. He's angry, confused and trusts neither the humans nor his fellow imps. He was in a place of honor in both realms and now he questions everything- his mission and his status. He is a liability. I believe that something must be done about him."

I hadn't the faintest idea what he thought I needed to do. "Something, like what?"

Randolph nearly laughed. "You're the great planner, the great thinker. What do you believe needs to be done to avoid his inquiry into our affairs? He is curious about why events are unfolding as they are. He may become a variable that we cannot control."

I told him the first thing that came to mind. "Silver or iron. The greatest danger is his using magic. If you can contain his ability to do that, that takes away one problem." I turned to Haglinda. "Can you somehow throw silver dust on him?" Silver and iron are magic inhibitors after all.

She looked at the ground and shook her head. "No, that would be dangerous. I would need to get too close to do that. I can cast a Silver Spell on him, though without getting close at all. Very easy. I've been operating here for over twenty years without anyone being the wiser. I can cast many hexes from afar."

I noted how funny it was that Vanna's accent kept changing. Which one was real? Who knew what her true form really was? Old woman, older woman? Animal, spirit, tree? She turned to me and patted my shoulder. "One of my gifts is clairvoyance. It's an imperfect gift, but I'm usually right when I get a sense. Hyacinth will come here in about five minutes no matter what my husband talks to her about. She will demand to know what we're discussing and why you've been acting strange lately. What I can't see is what you will tell her." I shrugged in reply. The truth is such a foreign tale for imps to tell.

Brutus looked at the three of us talking from across the

square. He was engaged in a conversation of his own with a lady in waiting. He lacked interest in it but she did not. Although the lady was enthralling and enchantingly beautiful, his eyes and ears were on us. Unfortunately for him our conversation could not be understood, not matter how hard he listened.

I turned back to Haglinda. "I can see he will be persistent. Can you cast the Silver Spell now?"

She nodded and pretended to tip an imaginary hat. "I already did."

I nodded a thank-you back and turned to Randolph. "Now we must bait him. His ability to interfere must be eliminated. I will draw him to the northern hill after this social hour is over." Looking over to where Hyacinth was, I saw that she detached herself from Gatekeeper Al, who was rambling.

In earnest, I asked Haglinda, "What is Hyacinth? You told me earlier that not even she knew. But you do."

Smiling as always she told me, "She is a good person inside. The truth about her, well, that is a longer story than we have time for. But I promise I will tell you when this is over."

"When what is over?" Hyacinth demanded. "Apologies to the present company," she made sure that Haglinda, Randolph, and the quickly arriving Al knew she was talking about them. "But Harold, you have been acting very strange lately, very secretive. And you've been saying very cryptic things which I can't decipher. Now you are conferring with others without me, as if I were uninvolved in your lifel. Something's either amiss, afoot, or afoul, and whatever it is, I deserve to know. I deserve to be trusted, if you love me." She crossed her arms crossly. Brutus watched our entire interaction in apparent dismay.

To answer Haglinda's earlier question, I told Hyacinth everything. Well, almost everything. I told her about the moonlock and the deal I made with Erumite. I told her how Sabrian and Syla knew of the deception and that I spoke to Monello with their blessing. I did not tell her that Randolph was a werewolf, that Haglinda and Al were Vanna and Warlocke, or that I was an imp. Most importantly, I did not tell her that in this peace, she would lose me.

The price of deception would be my humanity. It becomes me not, but, should it become me, I would lose my mortal coil and re-join my brother in blood.

As we spoke, I saw that instead of being furious with me, Hyacinth lit up. There was something of pride and also mischief in her eyes. She liked our game, and wanted to join in. "What can I do besides help boil the tea?" she asked eagerly.

"Just keep playing along." I looked over again at Brutus, whose quizzical stare was like an iron brand. "And take this satchel to your chambers. Within is everything we need for to-morrow." I removed it from my shoulders and handed it to her as stealthily as I could. I don't believe that Brutus saw me. I told Haglinda to remove the enchantment that made our conversa-tion indistinguishable from the outside.

With a loud whisper I said, "Alright, Hyacinth, go join your father and sister in the planning for tomorrow. Haglinda and Al, you may leave, thank you for your welcome input, and Randolph, it is always a pleasure to be in your company." I looked around and pretended not to see Brutus staring back at me. I pointed at myself with overly dramatic gesticulations. "I will go to the northern hill and commit the deed. Wish me well." They nod-ded and all wished me well in unison.

"Good luck," they said. Apple-Eater's curiosity must have gotten the best of him and he would follow me to see what I was up to. Curiosity affects cats and imps in much the same way.

I walked on the dirt path, the same one I walked when I was a newborn in this land. Now but a toddler, I continued on that path, never looking back, never wanting to catch Brutus follow-ing me. So I hadn't seen, but often heard, his pursuit. A twig snap, the rustling of leaves, the disturbance of a few birds. He was tailing me exactly as I wanted him to.

He is clever, but I was older and cleverer. I knew he'd give me a wide berth, quite a bit of distance between us. So when I finally reached the hillside, I stooped over to collect more moonlock. I hadn't needed it, but collecting it was for the sake of Brutus, not for me.

I took my time, gathered my thoughts as I gathered the spiny leaves. Just before I heard him coming closer, I was overwhelmed with an old familiar sensation. The undeniable thrill of a trick. I knew in my heart that it would never change. I would always be an imp at heart. But if I only did tricks for the sake of good, then I would never hate myself. Then I would be like the Horsefly of legend. If only I could be both human and imp at the same time.

I heard the heavy footfalls of a person who ate a lot of apple pie. He certainly was a lot taller in human form, I thought. He was husky and brave as a human and craven as an imp, almost a person of two entirely different personalities. He wore them like different hats. When you don't know yourself in your youth, you always wear different people before you discover which hat you like best.

"Harold! What are you up to? What's going on here? What are you, and everyone around here trying to pull?" He looked at the barren patch of field. His eyes widened in apparent horror and understanding. Although he might not have known what moonlock did, he was sure it was a poison of some kind.

"What is this? You can't take moonlock from this hill! You'll kill everyone, you took enough moonlock to--"

I relished the opportunity to finish his sentence for him. "To fell two entire nations at once." I crossed my arms in pretend victory. I stood up and placed the moonlock I gathered into my pockets.

He looked stunned. "The peace toast..."

"Yes, the peace toast."

His face changed from one of confusion to one of determination. "Well I'm not going to let you do that. I caught you in the act. This defiance will not be tolerated; both Sabrian and Erumite will be told, and perhaps they can be united in condemning you. And so I arrest you in the name of the royal house of Mansfield."

I smiled because I knew what he felt. He was a red imp like me after all. He was so much like I was in my youth. "And then you will be the hero, instead of me. They will love you for catching me, will they not? They will both appreciate your efforts."

He hesitated, but then grabbed his side-axe from its sheath. Before he could run and cut me down in one fell blow, Randolph, Haglinda and Al appeared from over the ridge of the hill. "What's this? You are all involved somehow! I'll get the Order and put a stop to this!" Haglinda rose one hand and Brutus fell to the floor, asleep.

She bent over his form, still clutching the axe. "I feel sorry for him. There is so much goodness there. He is lost, as are many. Why should he suffer the path of perdition?" She looked to me. "What do we do with him? He must be present for the toast."

I raised my eyes to her. "Let's give him some honey golden tea. He is lost, let us find him a way. Make him human. It's what he wants to be, anyway."

It was a bit of a shock for them to consider it. Would it be against his will? No. He should belong somewhere, I told them. And I always believed that the greatest place to belong was the kingdom of humanity. It would be a kindness to grant Brutus the gift of a life of potential, of possibility. One where he could choose his actions, even if he could not choose what future would befall him.

"He will forget everything," I said to them all. I turned to Haglinda and asked her to make him remember only the last six months, when he worked his way up from nothing to High Knight. "Let him remember his worth by allowing him to contribute to it." Brutus was expected as a member of the Order of

Nine to be present at the king's table. Therefore he needed to be fixed up and returned in a hurry. Vanna told me she would have to use some stronger ingredients, but that she'd have him back in time.

And so it was done. They spirited him away to the cottage that Al owned in the sparse part of town. I was left alone again, to walk the lonely dirt road back to the castle. It is in walking alone that one sometimes feels the greatest connection to the universe.

I walked and thought about so many things. I reflected on much, like a mirror of the world, as my mind wandered throughout the cosmos. How fascinating that by standing still, one can travel the infinite expanses of all that is real, and all that is not real, yet possible. To a realm like the future. One can think of it as far in advance as they wish, but it is not reality until it comes to pass. Should tomorrow come, will it be as it was in our dreams? Only we can make it so...

I thought of Hyacinth, and how perfect it would be to spend all my days on earth with her, until my last breath. But alas, she could never love me for what I truly am, and so I should spare her a life of such trouble. The thing with things, is that everything must end. No matter how short or how long, it shall be over someday, someway. But it is like a cloth, I thought. A drape, a fabric- it is not only how long it is which determines its worth, it is the quality of its stitching and the intricacy of the pattern it possesses. And Hyacinth had given me an immortal lifetime of happiness in five months, as silly as it is to say.

Suddenly I could not wait to see her again. My final act as her lover would be to pull off a great trick by her side, spiking the tea with moonlock. The impish part of myself was sated, and the human part as well. I traveled like a ghost down the road, so fully entrenched in my thoughts that I hadn't noted any of the scenery, and none of the other few people walking or riding that road. And in fact when you ignore something completely, it ceases to exist entirely, until you remember it.

Not remembering how I got there or how long it took- for time and space are both traversable without memory, I was immediately in her arms again, kissing and bestowing my love upon her.

We slept until nightfall, when the star-rise woke us. "It's almost time," she said. And she was right. There wasn't just tea to brew, but cookies and pies to bake, along with a spread of ham and cheese and olives to set. The king had dismissed his kitchen staff in order to allow me and Hyacinth to do what we must without any pestering by others. Therefore the burden of preparation fell squarely upon us. We only had eight or so hours before the arrival of dawn.

"Omelettes!" I said after a few hours of preparation. "Along with the traditional fare, we shall make potato omelettes." She laughed and caressed my face. Although imps rarely ate, they sometimes did. I recalled that Erumite loved potato omelettes with diced onion and bacon bits embedded into the potato. In a simple way, I thought that made him very philosophical. As if he understood that there were layers to everything.

We got to work. Hyacinth wore a formerly white apron, as did I. She looked like a baker's assistant. Now and never again, I thought sadly. Our synchronization was greater than that of the most intricate Swiss watches, which were either just recently invented or just about to be invented.

The energy we shared in our baking and the cooperation between us was like the very first night that I arrived in Mansfield. One thing about a circle is that you can follow it back to the beginning. If it veered off, it was no longer a circle, the perfect shape worshipped by the ancients.

Overnight, guardsmen had prepared tables and chairs for the feast, which would be held at the main square. All pubs in the land were emptied of cups, stools and benches. People donated furniture from their homes to ensure everyone had a seat and a place to drink and eat. Some donated wine and some donated cured meats and cheeses. When it came to celebrations, Mansfield was second to none. It was very serious business pertinent to everyone.

It was shaping up to be a relatively warm winter day. The previous dusting of snow had melted, and the rising sun shone with all its grandeur. A brighter sun there could not be, not even in the summer. I'd been pounding flour all night and all morning, and beating eggs and measuring sugar. Time flew faster than the great falcons trained by the Knight's falconers.

There were five enormous cauldrons brewing the tainted tarot root tea. It took four hours to bring them to a boil. Tarot root had a very distinct taste, a bitter dry sensation followed by a gradually sweetening aftertaste. It was a favorite among Mansfielders. It would completely overpower the leaves of acrid moonlock that were mixed in with the root.

The preparations may have felt like an eternity, but at last they were complete. The king entered the kitchen to wish us well before the imps arrived. Sabrian was in the fullest regalia that I'd ever seen him. Syla was by his side and was actually smiling. They both wore their crowns. He shook my hand with great strength. "Thank you, son. This could not have been possible without you. I have no words." Don't thank me yet, I thought. We need to succeed first.

He looked at Hyacinth in her apron, messy with flour and eggs, and I swore I saw pride in him. "Thank you as well, Hyacinth. You always make me so proud. Your gentle soul is something you must never lose, my dear. I have a question. It is up to the both of you- will you join us as ceremonial hosts at the king's table? I can have the kitchen staff finish up for you and serve everything. All you have to do is get ready."

Hyacinth and I looked at one another. "No thank you, King Sabrian. I think we'll be the meek ones today. As an old saying goes- 'To serve is the greatest honor.'"

Sabrian nodded in understanding and went out to the square with his High Knights in tow. I saw Brutus following the group; he seemed both placid and as bewildered as I was before I ate the prophetic grimmle-berry on the northern hill. Grimmle-berries are truly a wonderful thing. You could make cure-all elixirs from just a few berries. Last in the group of knights, Randolph nodded at me and raised a thumb to indicate everything was alright thus far. All was going according to plan.

The day was fast passing. The imps had arrived through the main Great Door, although they could have easily transported themselves in a reddish gray sea of foamy smoke. Gatekeeper Al let them in with that shining peasant smile of his, I'd imagine. I wondered if he boasted to Erumite how well he could read.

All was stormy- the fact that the day had finally come weighed too heavily upon me. There was more sadness than happiness in store for my future, I was certain of it. Today was the day I would save the woman I love and the family and people she holds dear. But it was also the day I'd lose her. As soon as Erumite fell asleep, I would be transformed into a red imp with charcoal gray eyes, a thing I would not want to impose on Hyacinth.

My true form, full of mischief and games and newfound weariness. Though I considered my own self very attractive, red is not everyone's color. In a way, I'd been fooling Hyacinth all along, if not on purpose then by withholding the truth.

The speeches commenced and I found myself in a dense mental fog, something that proved to me that I was still human. I'd never felt this way before. I was moving quickly to serve tea but time seemed to slow. I was moving through both time and space as if they were syrup and yet the rest of the world was unburdened with such setbacks. It sped on without any control.

The two houses had signed the treaty apparently when my mind was elsewhere. I hadn't heard any of what was said in the speeches, my sole focus being to assure that all the guests, young or old, imp or human, had a freshly brewed cup of poison tea.

Sabrian bellowed out a promise for a greater future of closer ties with newfound allies.

Erumite also spoke but briefly. He hadn't much to say apparently, except that he wanted to thank "Harold Baker. He is the humble man you have probably seen serving the best pies in town. I've heard his apple pie is phenomenal, and his tarot root tea is always a special brew." He raised his own cup. "He is too humble, in fact, to tell you that it was he that made peace between our two lands, acting on behalf of the great King Sabrian. His diplomacy is second to none, and in fact, Mansfield is the first nation that Monello has ever signed a peace treaty with. I invite him up here," he motioned to me to come up to him, "to stand alongside Sabrian and I give the peace toast."

And there was the rub. Erumite hadn't fully trusted me after all, and in that he proved very shrewd. Far more shrewd than most imps, which were easily susceptible to any and all tricks. Proof that nothing foul was afoot lay in my drinking my own brew. Perhaps he feared I was not to be trusted as the only person still awake. He called me out publicly to ensure I could not refuse him. If I did not drink, he would know something was wrong. Therefore, I did not refuse him, and in fact put on a smile as if I was flattered.

As I walked myself over to the dais where the kings stood, a flutter of questions arose in my mind. Why hadn't he trusted me? Did he suspect my true identity as Erubaca? Did the omelettes give it away? Did he have another angle, another countertrick up his sleeve? Only humans can have worries enough to choke an elephant.

Erumite's gray frame and scarlet eyes made him look ominous. I supposed he was always a bit ominous- there was always something in him less playful and more spiteful. Although fully immersed in daylight, there was a bit of him still in shadow; you could not make out all his features well. Maybe that is what magic looks like, a fuzzy possibility.

He was smiling. There was a big tray at the main table, from where he took a fresh cup of tea and handed it to me. We had extra teacups on every table. "To the man of the hour I ask, would you kindly give the peace toast?" I didn't think it possible, but his grin widened even more.

Accepting the cup politely, I bowed to him, and to Sabrian, and to the assembled masses, but not to the nobles. Not nearly the wordsmith my brother is, I simply said, "Teacups in hand, let us drink to peace and prosperity, and one hundred years of uninterrupted harmony!" Erumite winked at me as if to assure the harmony wouldn't be interrupted. I drank my toast, as did everyone else in near unison. I was amazed- the Mansfielders all drank their brew out of ritual and superstition, and the Monellons drank it to mark a new friendship. Diplomatic maneuvering via peace toast was a new game.

Looking particularly at the main dais, I saw that everyone took the lucky sip, even my brother. He seemed satisfied, and more than that- pleased that I'd led the way. He could trust me, since he could control me. Oh, nay to that. For I was born first and as tricksy as he is, I am simply more so.

One by one, everyone started to nod off. It hit Mansfield nearly all at once. The imps suddenly got groggy, but the Mansfielders suddenly went limp. Those standing fell, and some of those sitting wound up instead lying down. I fell down myself to complete the deception, hitting my shoulder hard on the ground to appear asleep.

Imps are more susceptible to the elixir than I had let on when earlier I spoke to my lone sibling. The effect of moonlock is a latent effect, but only by a few minutes. Assumably feeling tired, and understanding his mind would be lost to oblivion for the next hundred years, he commanded his men, "Everyone to Monello immediately!" Some groggy imps said, "I feel funny," "That tea didn't taste so good," and such things as they all disappeared in a great big puff of fluff.

Presumably they all arrived at the main door of Monello. I sincerely hoped they were able to go through it before falling into century-long slumber. I smiled. I pushed myself up with my good arm, rubbing my bad shoulder. It certainly smarted. Oh, mortality, what wonders you hold. Every cut, a cut closer to the end.

I stumbled towards Haglinda, who was seated with Al in blissful unawareness. They were on an ale-stained wooden bench that was delivered from The Blue Widower pub. Up until this moment I didn't know whether a witch and a wizard were able to be poisoned. I went to tap Haglinda by the shoulder, but before I could, Al said, "I wouldn't nary touch 'er, if'n I were you." She opened her eyes after peeking at me first.

"That was a nice little cat nap, eh? Now to wake the rest of these folk up. You've picked yourself quite a bit of berries for just such an occasion. All it takes is a little bit to make a big difference. Onward, Harold, this is your job, get to it." She whacked my bottom with a broom. Where had she gotten a broom from? I wondered.

I nodded. I hesitated. Grimmle-berries were the only antidote to moonlock. I ate a berry before the peace ceremony began. Sabrian and Erumite knew of the moonlock tea deception but only Sabrian knew of the grimmle-berry deception. Neither of them knew about my deal with Vanna whose sole condition was sincerity. Nor did Hyacinth.

"Except it's not going to be Harold any more is it? Once I wake the Mansfielders up with this berry juice, I won't be Harold. I'm going to be Erubaca again. And evermore. Lord of Monello. A king wearing a crown not meant for him. Erumite is a far better imp chieftain, if only he were less evil."

She nodded back in reply. "That's how it works I'm afraid. Every transaction has a cost, and for you the price of humanity is your identity. If you want to change yourself human, you must keep your promise. If you retract it, then you did not truly change yourself."

I closed my eyes. "It is for a good reason that I did this. They will awaken with one hundred years of peace from Erumite. Then when he wakes, I will retain my former rule from him. They are safe."

She'd kept on nodding at a steady pace. "Then it is worth the cost." She raised her hand invitingly, as if to say, "please then, wake them up."

I went to get the juice, but then turned back around. "I just have one more thing to ask of you, and it will be my last."

"Oh I don't think it'll be the last," she laughed and pointed to her eyes. "I'm clairvoyant, remember? I know."

"Then I don't need to ask..."

"About Hyacinth?" She remained seated with her hands folded on her lap. "No you don't need to ask. I'll tell you. She isn't human, as you secretly suspect. She is a Sprite."

Had I secretly suspected she wasn't human? Perhaps. Who else from their ranks was like her? However it takes more than just being one-of-a-kind to be human. They're all one of a kind in one way or another. Magic creatures are many of a kind. "I've heard of them but know practically nothing about them. What are sprites?"

She laughed heartily, exactly the kind of laugh you'd expect a witch to have. It was partway between cackle and genuine human laughter. It was infectious. Al simply smoked a pipe and looked on with his perennial bemused expression as she explained. "How could you, above all others, not know what a sprite is? I won't give you the particulars of her life because it's not for me to do that. But I will educate you a little on sprites my lad.

"When imps, who are all male, fall in love with women of other kinds, the imps always leave their own kind and join with the female. But they don't only produce male children. Male children of imps are of course, imps. And female children--"

CHAPTER 6

"Are sprites!" I concluded in victory.

"Well, naturally," she said. "Sprites are sent off to their own queendom, Monella, when they are little. Like imps, they don't know their parents, for their parents live wherever the mother came from. Imps and Sprites rarely if ever meet. But I'd like to think that when they do, it's fate." She winked. Her hands were still folded. Her posture on the bench made her look like she was about to feed bread to pigeons.

"To make a long story that's none of your business short, Hyacinth came to me in her youth, much like you did. She was younger than you were at the time. Maybe a hundred years old, I don't remember. For whatever reason, she desired to be human as well. I granted her request and she awoke in the forest to be found by Ophelia and Sabrian. The rest is history."

I could see Hyacinth further down in the square. She'd fallen on top of a redheaded bloke, who looked like he hit his head on the way down. I happily noted that it was the same bloke who'd spurned my friendship on my first day in town.

I turned back to Haglinda. "What did you do with my talisman?"

"I thought you said you only had one thing to ask of me?" she pretended to huff. "Do you see how clairvoyant I am?" She paused. "It's with me, in my pocket. But not for long, Harold. No human life lasts forever and mine has already been too long. What do you want me to do with it when I'm gone?"

I hadn't considered it, but I didn't want it. At least not yet. As long as it was in good hands for a century, there was no need to worry about it until then. I considered it for a moment. "Give it to Brutus. Whether human or imp he craves to matter, to be worth something, to be trusted. It's why he relished being both a Mansfield knight and a Monello spy. It wasn't about ideology or allegiance, but about meaning something to someone or some group of people. Life is like that at his age."

Haglinda looked into the sky. "It is like that at any age. To matter is the greatest endeavor of every life, no matter how long or how short. And it is the greatest gift mortality gives us. Mortality gives us the opportunity to hurry up about it." She took a deep breath with her eyes closed. "So what will you do? You can stay here and give them the antidote, or you can leave them here to sleep while you carry on as a human being somewhere else."

Looking back at a sleeping Hyacinth, who taught me love, I determined that action through love is the only way to truly matter in this life. "I will pay the price of humanity," I told Haglinda. "Even if I must lose it."

EPILOGUE

Hans and Adelaide were fast asleep from listening to my endless story, as was Poppa. Bruella's cauldron had fully boiled hours ago, and the potatoes within must have turned into mash on their own. She was still politely acknowledging me, with either feigned or actual attention; I could not tell after all this time. Hansel was stewing with drunken odor but his eyes were still on me. They both must have been hungry. Where were my manner, overstaying my welcome like that?

"The rest is another long story for another long night, and perhaps I will tell you another time," I said, pretending to just notice the lateness of the hour. The snow had stopped falling and the wind had calmed down.

"Oh, you're always welcome here," Bruella told me with what I believed was sincerity. Hansel nodded, perhaps unable to make any other motion. I took these as signs to finally leave.

"One thing." At the door, I turned and looked back at Hansel. "Before I go I wanted you to know something. You are an heir of Brutus, and you descend from noble hearts. Brutus as a human being was a kind, just, compassionate person, full of valor and chivalry. He lived out the rest of his days as a good man.

147

That is where you come from, Hansel. And that is how my talisman fell to you. Guard it well, as well as your forbears did." It was a request but also a warning. It needn't have been.

As soon as I left the small dilapidated cottage, I made myself transparent. Transparency is a fun trick. You can see people's darkest thoughts and actions, when they believe no one is looking. I peered through a large crack in the door, at Hansel slowly reaching into his pocket. Instead of pulling out my ring, he discovered he had a five pound piece of king's gold. The ring, of course, was with me, as I'd switched it immediately.

Though drunk off my wine, he of course sought me out, bellowing curses loudly into the dark forest. But he couldn't find me. I was already happily walking on my way back. To you. My Hyacinth. And now with me prostrate on the floor and this ring in my hand I ask you with all my heart, "Will you finally marry me?"